The Key to
REAL HAPPINESS

The Key to
REAL HAPPINESS

Stephen Knapp

Ocean Books Pvt. Ltd.
ISO 9001:2015 Publishers

Published by
Ocean Books (P) Ltd.
4/19 Asaf Ali Road,
New Delhi-110 002 (INDIA)
e-mail: info@oceanbooks.in

ISBN 978-81-8430-504-3
THE KEY TO REAL HAPPINESS
by Stephen Knapp

Edition
2026

Price
₹ 300.00 (Rupees Three Hundred only)

Printed at
Shree Sai Printers, Sahibabad

Preface

One of my biggest desires is to see that everyone in the world can be happy. I have traveled through various parts of the world and seen people in all kinds of situations, both pleasant and very miserable conditions. Some are quite content, even happy, while others are struggling for all their necessities. And I'm one of those people who would like to change things for the better. I've dreamed of building a huge house and take in all of the orphans, all of the abused women, all of the homeless old men, and anyone else who needs shelter and protection and decent facilities in which to live, and put them there so that they could feel loved, cared for, and sheltered. Unfortunately, that is a dream that may be a long way off since I hardly have that kind of financial facility. However, in the meantime, I can still write this book to show the way people can be happier.

After all, if there is one thing I have learned in life, it is not merely a matter of giving everyone nice material facility that will make them happy. There is more to it than that. Some people that have plenty of everything are still miserable. And I have seen those who had nothing that were quite happy. So it is also a matter of consciousness and attitude that can make the greatest difference. And we are in greater control of that than we often think. And that is why I am writing this book.

As it has been said, a person may be in hell, but by remembering God they can feel like they are in heaven. And a person can be in heaven, but by forgetting God, they may soon feel like they are in hell. The point is that happiness is a matter of adjusting one's consciousness. Without this, material facility can only help to a basic degree.

So I do not have the money to take in everyone that needs help. But I can give them this information by which they can begin to adjust their own perception, their own consciousness, by which happiness is more accessible, more readily attainable. It is indeed a matter of consciousness, a state of mind, and a matter of perception. That is what we need to direct in the right way.

Contents

1
Getting Started to Find Our Way

We all want to be happy, right? Why else do we want to live in this world? And many people are looking for the key to real happiness, and most find variable forms of it. However, no one can find true and lasting happiness until they realize who and what they really are, and the true purpose of this life and this creation. These have been some of the greatest mysteries of the world, and many have tried to get a glimpse into this understanding.

The paths to various levels of such realizations are many, but the goal has been reached by few. Fortunately, some of those who have reached this goal have shared their knowledge with others, and have helped to point the way. I was blessed enough to meet such a person and was shown one of such paths. Now I want to share what I have learned with you. So please listen carefully.

This book is not merely about how we need to more fully appreciate what we have, although that always helps. Naturally, we all need to look around and count our blessings and realize that things are not as bad as they could be, or that we have a good situation. But what this book is about is how we can widen our perspective by changing our consciousness.

There are millions of ways to proceed in this world in one's attempt to find various levels of happiness. And they all have different results, some obvious, and some much less than we would hope for. So which one would be the most efficient, the best, is the answer for which we should look.

This book will act as a link to the many avenues that provide varying levels of happiness, amusement, or preoccupation. Beyond that is the path to real happiness. Many people become quite satisfied on one or more of these avenues. Other people, however, need more than this. There are those who feel that having followed a particular avenue to material happiness, no matter how beautiful the road may have seemed, has merely lead them to shallow results. Or even to a sort of prison or dead end in which they feel stuck or disillusioned with no means of escaping or changing the situation. This book can act as a viewing station from where we can see the ultimate end of the particular avenues to material happiness that this universe offers. It also provides the means by which we can go beyond the results of these worldly avenues for something far more important, far more pleasurable, and far more realistic, provided you have the capability to understand the true nature of this world and the true identity of yourself.

The material world can be compared to a fancy trap that we fall into. Once we receive a human body, a whole field of activities in this dimension opens that provides us a choice of many directions we can take, each one leading to another area we can investigate for the pursuit of material enjoyment and emotional fulfillment. As anyone can see, there are many interesting things around us, all kinds of activities, goals, pleasures, as well as intrigue and problems, some of which can attract us and occupy many years of our lives. Nonetheless, there is another secret about this place. That secret, therefore, is to find the means, the path that can take us beyond mere material amusements and preoccupations, and back to our real spiritual nature, our actual home, to our genuine, eternal and blissful position. That is where the real happiness can be found.

Finding real happiness on this higher level is also like a power. It is a power because it is totally individualistic. No one and nothing can take it away once you have it. That spiritual happiness is also universal because it is the energy that pervades the universe, and the essence within everyone. It is natural because it is our pure state of being. It does not rely on the constant catering to the senses, which can never go on indefinitely. It is what everyone is looking for. It is the only thing that can provide a lasting feeling of total fulfillment because it is connected to our real identity, beyond the body, mind or intellect. So when we are not in that state of individual and independent happiness, then something unnatural is keeping it from us, or interrupting that flow of natural joy within us. Getting free from those disturbances that intrude into our spiritual focus is what we can learn to do.

As we can see, for most people, much of our happiness in this material dimension is based on solving all of the problems that occur in order to make our lives smoother, more peaceful, and, thus, happier. Then when we get the chance to take it easy, we enjoy watching a sunset, a walk on the beach, a ride on the bicycle, or some form of entertainment. But merely trying to enjoy our leisure between solving problems is not real happiness. Neither is giving pleasure to our temporary mind and senses real happiness. It is more of a preoccupation while our life drifts by. The goal in this life is to find the clues that will show us the right path to complete freedom, wherein lies the real happiness for which we always search. It is on that level of reality where we can be who we really are as spiritual beings. Otherwise, as spiritual entities in a material world, we are like fish out of water. No matter what kind of material facility we have, or how much we get, it is nonetheless an incompatible situation. It never really fits us nor gives us what we need to be truly happy and fulfilled, and to attain the freedom to be who and what we really are as unlimited spiritual beings. That will only happen when we begin to regain our natural position in connection with our spirit, or the spiritual dimension.

Even if you have never been interested in such topics, this book can open your eyes to possibilities, the likes of which you may have never known or ever pondered before. Quite honestly, that is exactly what happened to me. I was simply looking for a few answers, a higher level of understanding for what to do with my life, and before I knew it, I was being shown such lofty levels of seeing the world, and higher realms of existence and consciousness like I had never known nor previously considered. Then I knew there was no turning back. It was as if a door had been opened to me that allowed me to see through the veils of illusion that are the basis of worldly existence for most people. Suddenly, for me everything changed instantly. The world was not the same, nor was I. Everything came together and made sense. No longer was the world my problem. Other people were not my problem. What I had done in the past was not my problem. It was only my point of view that was the difficulty. It was merely the way I viewed myself and things around me that was incorrect. And that was determined by my upbringing, or by the knowledge, education, and information I had been presented or acquired in my life. Or maybe I should say that it was the lack of the right kind of information that had kept me within the confines of the same illusions as everyone else-everyone else except for those few sages who had taken the path to go beyond the illusions that restrict and confine so many of us.

Therefore, my writing of this book is also a display of gratitude for those sages and masters who have taken the path to such higher levels of consciousness and reality, and particularly to those who have taken the additional responsibility to try to show the rest of humanity the way, in spite of the lack of interest that much of this society seems to have. Especially for my own friend and teacher who took me in and made such sacrifices to help and guide me. For him I write this book. He had also ordered me to help others. And I certainly hope this book can do this for you. In this way, only by helping you can I help myself.

□

2

Are You Really Happy?

So, are you happy? Are you truly content? Or are there many things that you wish you could change? Do you wish you had a better job? A better girlfriend or boyfriend, wife or husband? A better place to live? A nicer car? Are there other changes you anticipate in your life which should give you happiness after having accomplished or achieved them?

Let's face it, if you are still hoping for happiness, it means you do not have it. Sure, sure, maybe things are OK and not too bad. Maybe you need to appreciate what you have more than you do. We all need to do that. Yet, maybe you are still hoping for improvements, substantial changes, and so on. However, just trying to be satisfied with what we already have does not mean we have to stagnate, or merely act like everything is just fine. And if you have not found the spontaneous or self-sufficient happiness that you would like by now, maybe you do not know where to find it. So where are we supposed to look?

In order to know where to find genuine happiness, we must also discern where not to look. So let us consider this. Did you know that the World Happiness Survey, as of 2001, placed the United States at 46th among the happiest countries in the world? This is not so good. The United Kingdom was only 32nd. Yet India was recorded as being second on the list as having the happiest people in the world. Now when you think that we have got more facility and comforts than most countries, why aren't the people of America happier? When we evaluate this, it appears that the people of the most advanced countries often are the least happy.

One problem is that most of these "advanced" countries propose a lifestyle emphasizing consumerism and the acquisition of wealth and possessions as the basis of happiness. It is the concept that happiness lies within the control of one's external situation, or surrounding oneself with everything he or she needs in order to pamper the mind and senses with stimulation and ease of living. It is this western society that stresses that happiness can be found in the next purchase of the latest appliance or gizmo, or a bigger house, or whatever else you think you need. This idea leads one down a wrong path. Now from where did this idea come? Thinking that this is what brings happiness often merely leads one to stress and anxiety, the pressure of pursuing one's material goals, which is actually another form of misery no matter how slight it may be. Being in stress is not happiness. And it can lead to more serious diseases, such as headaches, high blood pressure, back pain, emotional problems, heart attacks, which can continue to lead to other social difficulties, all of which decrease one's duration of life. It is for this reason that the most prosperous countries seem to have the least happiness. Therefore, we need to understand that even on the most basic material level, where there is the least stress one can find the most happiness.

It is often seen that accepting intentional or voluntary simplicity is a way to attain a stress-free lifestyle, in which case happiness is easier to attain. More money does not mean more happiness. It may help attain some freedom. But freedom for what? If you have the financial freedom to waste time and resources on unnecessary purchases or a frivolous lifestyle, then what good is the extra money? It often only creates more problems in such a case, especially when the money begins to run out. Then some people start getting so upset that their money is getting scarce that they will do all kinds of embarrassing or even compromising or illegal activities to try to get more money.

Furthermore, if we look closely we can see that consumerism is, basically, another form of selfishness displayed in our attempts to meet all our demands for personal pleasure. We can see that the importance placed on this can lead to additional breakdowns, not only of our health from feelings of pressure and stress, as mentioned earlier, but also in the breakdowns of our environment, our resources, families, as well as social culture. As we pursue the race to maintain all of our material standards that we have become accustomed to, or that we desire, we tend to adopt the attitude that we want to lead a life of ease and facility at whatever cost. Even at the expense of losing our environment, clean air and water, and so on, so that polluting factories can produce what we think we want. In other words, we begin to lose our natural resources and all that we need to maintain ourselves and provide for a peaceful life. And without peace, there can be no happiness.

Happiness in this sort of environment also seems to be based on the anticipation or hope that something new is going to come along and change everything. You will want to get a better position or job, a better paying occupation, a more exciting partner, a bigger house or apartment, and so on. We think that when we achieve such things, then everything will be different--better. Then when that does not happen, happiness is missing, and disappointment follows. Or if you do acquire such things in your attempt to be happy, in many cases you spend much of your life taking care of problems to maintain what you have. If something or someone breaks down or needs attention, you have to stop and take care of it. Many people are often so busy with their numerous affairs and problems that they have no time to really ask whether they are truly happy. They are simply too preoccupied with everything.

Similarly, when you have a family, you also need to attend to the demands of others. To take care of the needs of your loved ones may certainly bring a type of joy, to be needed by them and watch them grow. Yet, often times the desires and demands of your family do not cease but increase. They are always in need or in want of something more because of the philosophy of consumerism that is all around us. Thus, rather than spending time enjoying life and being content, you often are neglecting yourself for the benefit of someone else, and merely going from one problem to the next trying to take care of the needs or demands of others. The point is that you cannot really enjoy your life or what you have if you are always struggling to maintain it or have no time to appreciate it.

It reminds me of the Taoist expression that when you have a jug, it is the emptiness inside which makes it useful. If it becomes too full, there is nothing else you can do with it. Similarly, our life is useful when we have the time to reflect and be content. If we are too busy, what else can we do with our lives when we have no time? I remember when my friends and I were 19 and 20 years old. We thought being 30 was ancient and so far away that it would take forever for us to reach that age. Now that I am way beyond 30, I look back and realize that it did not take that long to get to where I am now. It all goes by much quicker than you think. Have you ever noticed that the busier you are, the faster time goes by, and the more rapidly your life disappears? It may be time to slow down.

It has been found that in poor countries, a slow and simple agrarian lifestyle often leads to higher levels of happiness rather than the lifestyle of being overly busy working and acquiring an assortment of objects and possessions to pamper or thrill the mind and body. I have been to India several times, and many people seem to be oblivious to the fact that they are poor. But poor by whose standards? They are often happier and friendlier than people in the West while making the best of whatever they have. We may have so much material facility, such as nice house, car, clothes, money, etc., but if we lack inner contentment, then we are truly poor. This would indicate that the real happiness we are looking for is really inside us, not outside. We just have to reconnect with who we really are and reach that happiness within. When we do that, we carry that connectedness, that self-assuredness wherever we go, in whatever we do, in whatever happens. When we can do that, we will attain self-sufficient happiness.

Therefore, the above information would suggest that real happiness is not found in the acquirement of temporary objects, prizes or possessions.

Naturally, there can be a thrill to achieve something significant in life, whether it be a better occupation, passing a tough exam, or taking yourself physically to the limit and winning in an athletic sport of some kind after months or years of practice. These can all be sources of personal pride and happiness. But these all come and go. This does not mean that you should not do them. It means not to get caught up in making your whole life evolve around them. After all, we all retire at some point. Our big new job will not last forever. The exam we passed may only give way to newer tests later on. And the physical sport that we are so good at today will be done better by some younger person in due time.

What does this mean? It means to take pleasure in them only for the personal progress and maturity they help you make, not merely for the state of mind they produce, knowing full well that the mental platform is flickering. What may feel great today may not give the same thrill later, or may even become boring. It also means not to make your whole identity something that you know will change with age. You cannot help but change, and you must be malleable to that aspect of life. Your identity as a baseball star, a movie personality, a hot model, a music icon, or any other kind of celebrity or position, may be recorded in history, but someone younger will at some point come along and take your place, along with your share of the glory, and no doubt for more money. So do not feel resentful, nor should you think that is where to find real happiness that does not fade, because all material things diminish with time.

The point is that being truly happy does not need the acquirement of something. Happiness that depends on the increase of temporary comforts, possessions or position is an illusion. People get married for happiness. They pursue a career for happiness. Or they buy a big house for happiness. Then they get divorced for happiness. Or they quit their job for happiness. Or they move into another place for happiness. Happiness remains very elusive through such endeavors if you have not already found it within you. You need to be happy right here and now, in your present situation, in your Self. Otherwise you may never be fulfilled.

Happiness is basically a state of mind. Happiness depends more on one's disposition and outlook. Only by connecting to your real identity, deeper than merely the body and mind, can one reach real happiness because that is where such happiness is always found. In this way, very little is needed to have a happy life. It is all within yourself. Thus, we can attain a state of being satisfied with what we have without being anxious to attain all our temporal desires, without worrying about the future, and without concerning ourselves with unnecessary hopes and fears. When you are really and naturally happy from within, everything else that you accomplish can be viewed as icing on the cake, an extra sweetness to life. But such external activities are not where true happiness lies.

For example, there is an old Buddhist saying: If you have a problem you cannot solve, why worry about it? If you have a problem you can solve, then why worry about it? So if our happiness depends on things we cannot control, we will always experience worry and despair. Thus, happiness comes from ceasing to worry about that which is beyond our influence, or even that within our control.

Let's say that someone says something critical or harsh about you and you feel bad because of it. Or maybe you get angry. You then make the arrangement to face them and correct the situation. And if a simple discussion with them rectifies the situation, all well and good. But maybe you want to do more than this. Maybe you even take them to court if it is serious enough. Once you do this and if you win, you feel vindicated, having protected your honor. Maybe the person does indeed deserve a lesson. However, if you know yourself truly, that is more important than to care how others see you. When you are established in your true inner identity and connected to your real Self, you will care little about defending your honor or how others perceive you or what they may say. You will go on with your life, content with who you are and will care little about how others understand you, especially if they do not care enough to really get to know you anyway. Thus, you will not lose your state of happiness just because someone else has said something bad about you. This is the importance of being connected with your true identity and inner Self. This is what we need to do.

The only reason why people cannot attain their inward spiritual bliss right here and now is because they put too much focus on their external situation and what they feel they need and how to get it. Or they focus on the problems that they think they have. Actually, what people need in order to be happy is right inside them, at all times, regardless of whatever trials and challenges may happen outside and around them. As I have always said, it is not what happens to you, but it is how you perceive it and how you react or respond to it that makes the difference. We have to understand that happiness and distress is a constant flow in material life. We are affected by it only if we identify with it. One has to learn to rise above that by connecting with your true self, or higher Self. So how do we do that? That is what we are going to learn in the following chapters.

□

3

Your Thoughts Create Your Future

One thing I want to do right now before we go any farther is to explain some information that many people can use. I have said earlier in this book that happiness can be, essentially, a state of mind, or a particular outlook on life. But often times we can observe how our mind is affected by what goes on around us, sometimes by things which do not matter that much. Nonetheless, we get sucked into thinking that it matters a lot. Thus, our thoughts and consciousness become absorbed in negativity, which can greatly affect our disposition, or the way we relate to people, and pave the way for a less than happy future. So what do we do about this?

In the course of our lives we may be bombarded with negative thoughts, energies or scenarios that may come not only from within us but also from outside ourselves or from others. All around us is a network of people, businesses, governments, publications, movies and music, all telling us what has been going on, or what they think is best for us, what we should buy and do, or what we should think about something. As soon as we tune into the radio, television, or open a magazine, it all jumps out at us. Our minds can be receptacles of these thoughts and desires, or even criticisms, which then become a part of our own consciousness if we are not careful. These thoughts are like electrical currents which, although unseen, can be felt and produce internal effects.

As we become objects of such energies, these thoughts and vibrations that we are exposed to can affect the quality of our lives, goals, and the way we think about ourselves. Therefore, to ensure our own success and happiness in life, we must learn how to protect ourselves from these outside influences of negative or materialistic thoughts or actions that may come from or are caused by others. To avoid being overly influenced by the media, we need to make sure we have the time to raise our own consciousness enough to discriminate between what is truly needed for our own happiness, and what is merely the affects of external persuasions that are being dumped on us by outside forces that simply want our money, our vote, or to convince us to act in a certain way, or even to be a silent peon that simply cooperates with the mass consciousness and is not noticed by anyone. It is not easy to avoid the system that continually indoctrinates people, even if on the subtle level, to act in certain ways or spend their money on particular items. Once you are locked into this network, which produces the materialistic mindset, it is most difficult to become self-sufficiently happy. The system makes you think that your happiness has to be according to the dictates and standards set by others, whether it is your teachers, parents, fellow employees, company supervisors, politicians, or what you see on television and in magazines. You will have to be able to rise above this influence to take a good look at who you are, otherwise life could carry you along without you ever knowing your true potential and spiritual possibilities. Do not be afraid to step outside the mainstream, even if you maintain a low profile in society. Some of the most powerful people on the planet, and the most happy, are those that the world never knows. Their spiritual discipline keeps them from being observed except by a very few.

On a personal level, the more prominent you become in society, the more people will focus their thoughts and energies on you. Some people may simply be envious of you. Or if you are something like a politician, people may blame you for their problems. However, everyday misunderstandings will always develop between people. So, to help protect ourselves from verbal or psychic attacks from others, practice raising the consciousness of those who try to attack you. First, remember there is no attack unless you accept it. See these attacks as calls for help, and review what you will do or say the next time in order to help your would-be attackers. This will protect you and help them as well.

Throughout the day, notice how every word you hear and every action you witness is either an expression of love or a cry for love. This love is the essence of happiness. And in all actions that people may perform, to find the means by which they can love and be loved is their primary purpose, whether they realize it or not. Besides food, shelter and clothing, it is the greatest need of all living beings. It is the essential nature of the soul, and the basis of everyone's outer actions and desires. So remember to respond to the calls for love with love. Practice being a loving presence for everyone, and observe any changes that occur in yourself and those around you.

Also, practice carrying your own atmosphere with you. In other words, keep that loving presence with you. For example, meditate on being in a sacred place and the feeling or consciousness you have while there. Now be absorbed in and project that atmosphere out around you wherever you are, and to others nearby. As such, you can be your own temple. In this way, when around people of negative energy, you can concentrate on sharing your own positive energy rather than absorbing theirs. In this way, you also create a protective barrier around yourself while maintaining a kind and friendly attitude. The primary objective in such a situation is to give them more of your energy, your understanding, and your essence rather than accepting theirs. You can even imagine light emanating from within you and encompassing them, clearing and cleansing all undesirable energy from the environment.

Practice being unaffected by the envy of others, whether it is directed at you or anyone else. You will gradually learn to be concerned about their welfare but undisturbed by their behavior. Bless those who wish you misfortune, or who are simply lost in their anger and bitterness toward the world in general. This blessing reduces their ability to harm you, because your positive energy counteracts their negative energy. Remember to apply the science of love in all circumstances. If, however, you react to their negative energy with your own negative thoughts, you simply increase the negativity and unbalanced disposition of your own consciousness, and in the surrounding atmosphere. This makes you even more vulnerable to increased receptivity of low energy thoughts and verbal or psychic attacks. It also increases your susceptibility to reversals in life and the manifestations of your own worries and fears. In other words, negative energy builds upon more negative energy, with which you thus surround yourself.

The highest protection we can provide for ourselves is a solid sense of love and compassion for ourselves and others. We need to think and act in dynamic and positive ways and hold a love for ourselves in order to feel a sense of completeness and happiness in who we are. Without enough love from within, you will lack the necessary armor to protect yourself from the relentless attacks of negative energy. Strong inner love will allow you to deflect such harmful energy, or to even transmute it so that it has no destructive effects. Therefore, always remember to put up a shield of love for your protection, keeping in mind that in order to love others, you need to love yourself first. The more you understand your true spiritual identity, and your connection with the Supreme, the easier it will be to love your Self.

This love is a way of balancing our consciousness and *karma*, the reactions of past actions. When our consciousness is out of balance, it means we must continue to learn how to get it equipoised again. Holding emotions like anger, envy, the urge to get back at someone, etc., all are signs of an unbalanced mind and consciousness. Justice and balance in one's *karma* is the equalization of all energies, including our thoughts, words and deeds. All of these together create impressions in the mind which then helps form our consciousness and produce our emotional predispositions, character traits, memories, and even unexplainable fears. Any imbalances in our consciousness, along with our *karma*, create many instances and lessons that we are forced to endure in order for us to gain the necessary insights to once again stabilize our consciousness. So what lies ahead for us, and especially what we think of at the time of death, is determined by such factors as our attractions, repulsions, how we behave in this life, and how we handle the way others treat us. This also may be influenced by our previous *karma*, or how we have handled previous tests and situations in the past. This all affects our state of consciousness at the time of death, which guides our soul in a particular direction into the next life.

To help control this aggregate impression in the mind in order to balance our consciousness for inner peace, we need to bring in higher and positive thoughts. This is called controlling the lower self by the higher Self. We can purposely change our thinking from negative to positive. For example, instead of thinking about how someone did something mean or hateful, we can conclude such thinking and begin focusing on the good things in our lives and be more loving.

The reason why this is important is that thoughts are things, energies that can vibrate on different levels, both high or low. It is a person's free will that determines how such energy will be used and at what vibratory level it will operate. The intent of one's thought is what determines this vibratory level, and the ultimate outcome of one's actions, which then helps create our future.

If our, or anyone's, thoughts are based on goodwill or loving intentions, those thoughts carry a high vibration. If such thoughts have a low or selfish intent, they will carry and spread that low energy. Keeping our intentions in a spiritual direction will always help maintain a high vibratory level of our consciousness, and help protect us from those who have an ulterior motive, even if it is the vibration of the images and words that come over the radio, television, magazines, newspapers, etc.

For example, if we worry about something all the time, it is a way of focusing on a particular thing or idea that will manifest in that way. Thus, worry is a prayer for something one does not want. To avoid undesirable outcomes, we must learn to control our thoughts, especially when we are under emotional stress. Stress and emotion are forms of thought energy which fuel the creation of the image being held in our minds. Instead of worrying, we can replace such negative energy and thought-forms with a visual image of the desired outcome. In this way, we can help that positive image manifest rather than the unwanted one by feeding emotional energy into the thought form you fear. As we get into the habit of energizing only the positive, our thoughts, words and deeds will automatically reflect the higher state of mind. They will, in effect, stop creating new negative *karma* because they will no longer generate energy that has to be rebalanced, and their positive energy will begin paying off some of the debits in our past bad *karma*, which itself can manifest as unbalanced or negative thoughts.

Even if you cannot control your thinking, as when you might be in emotional duress, then begin acting in positive ways, such as focusing on the care and concern for others who may be in a more problematic situation than yourself. Or even begin praying for the benefit of those less fortunate. Your thoughts and consciousness will immediately begin to change into that which is positive and uplifting.

The decision to think and function in a positive mode is the first step in transmuting energy to a higher level, which means raising its vibratory rate. Energy transmuted in this way attracts even more positive energy, producing a snowball effect which assists in furthering the creation of a new, happier and more desirable future. Controlling your thought energies in this way can make a difference between success and failure, not only with yourself, but those with whom you associate or work. If you want to help yourself as well as your work partners, or even your enemies, you must practice this form of controlling your thoughts. Otherwise, if you are continually being negative or harboring low levels of thinking, it may be better for those around you to work separately if they wish to be successful, or at least happy. The reason is that you are not contributing to their success or desired future, and neither to your own. This is why transmuting your thoughts to higher and more positive levels of consciousness can determine the difference between success or failure, not only in business, but also in health, happiness, peace of mind, and in reaching your dreams, and certainly in making any spiritual progress.

One of the ways negative energy can harm you is when you harbor it for long periods of time and it accumulates and becomes lodged in your body. These energies are dense and vibrate at a level too low for the body to process and release. As a result, they become blocked and crystallized, manifesting at best as diminished stamina, loss of energy, or decreased mobility. Thus, stagnant, unreleased negative energy can eventually have a harmful effect and produce dis-ease. However, such energies can be released from the body and our consciousness through methods such as forgiveness, prayer, meditation, or through conscious transmutation, as described above.

Modern medicine is slowly accepting the reality of "mind over matter," recognizing the power of the mind to influence the functioning of the human body. Therefore, it is in everybody's best interest to learn to release low energy by first moving it out of the physical body, then out of the conscious and subconscious mind, and the etheric body and aura. People can accomplish this by a conscious release of old grudges and resentments, or by deliberately shattering it into smaller bits and pieces in order to make the release more effortless.

In addition, strive to "love your enemies," as hard as that may be. Pray for them because such prayers decrease their power to hurt you, and the high energy released in the process will be returned to you in kind. Remember, everyone acts, positively or negatively, to express love or call for love.

Monitor your thoughts carefully. As you think of someone lovingly, angrily or lustfully, note how that person becomes unconsciously affected by your thoughts. Remember, thoughts are things. They are composed of the same electrical, spirit-based energy that pervades the rest of the universe. Thoughts have substance and power, and the more emotional energy people give them, the faster they will become a reality. This is part of the process of meditation, bringing into your life that which you are meditating on. The spoken word has the same force and creative energy. Therefore, those who learn to control their thoughts and words will control their future. Since humans are constantly creating, the only issue is whether they are being conscious creators or unconscious ones, and, thus, creating a positive future or one that is negative.

So, think of plans that can assist the whole of humanity. Raise your level of consciousness. To understand that you are a co-creator is to be in harmony with the universe, acting as a servant of and co-worker with the Divine. If you fail to appreciate this reality, you can become destructive and are responsible for causing even more chaos in society or disharmony in your life. You can easily look around and recognize many others who have this same problem and create the described effects. So do not be one of them. The choice is yours, and so are the consequences. You manifest what you hold in your consciousness.

Remember, thought is energy that can create your future. Begin thinking of how bright your future will be and begin creating the bright future for yourself that you have a right to. Then just do it!! Stick to your plan to make it a reality, and do not give up. Do not doubt yourself, and do not become confused. Always go forward toward your goal. And choose your association carefully, which means only work with and depend on those who will help you reach your goals. You can succeed!!!

□

4

Starting to Get Connected to Your Higher Self

Happiness is a part of our spiritual nature. In Sanskrit, that nature is called *sat-chit-ananda*. The word *sat* means eternal. The soul is eternal and its natural tendencies are also eternal. The word *chit* means knowledge, especially the higher spiritual knowledge that is connected with our eternal nature. In our natural and fully realized spiritual position, we are full of knowledge, and we know what to do and how to do it--in other words, no confusion. The word *ananda* means full of bliss. Again, the eternal, awakened nature of the soul is to always be full of happiness. It is always within us. The problem with attaining this bliss is that before we are fully connected with our higher Selves, we search for it outside of us. Thinking our inner joy comes from something external only contributes to our confusion and frustration. It adds to our misidentification of who and what we really are, and what we really need. The fact is, our body alone cannot make us happy. It is a machine in which we exist, although we may feel fairly pleased with it when we are healthy and in good shape. Likewise, our mind alone cannot make us happy. What we seek is deeper than that. Finding the happiness within may not always be easy, but it is impossible to find it elsewhere.

To be convinced that our search for happiness should be in things outside ourselves is what shuts us out from finding the happiness already within us. What value is our happiness if we must work hard and struggle for it? That merely means we are looking in the wrong direction. Sure, maybe we do have to work hard, but that should not be the cause of either our happiness or distress. We attain happiness from what we learn, what we accomplish, and the experience or personal progress we derive from it. This is especially powerful when what we do is connected with how our inner Self is revealed.

Our spiritual nature may come out of ourselves and manifest in many ways. For example, on a most basic level, someone may be born artistic, and art may play a great part in the ways one expresses himself and attains happiness. Someone else may be born with a natural tendency for cooking and feel completely content in the kitchen. Another may feel best by learning nursing and helping others who are suffering. There are so many ways in which such inherent abilities and talents may lead us toward what we are meant to do, and the happiness for which we look. Thus, a key to happiness is finding our talents and being able to do them. Without that, we may pass through life lethargically.

An important point is that happiness and enthusiasm come from doing what you like, liking what you do, and feeling that you are contributing to the betterment of others by doing it. Or that you are providing something that is needed by the community which is appreciated. This is connected with feeling happy by serving others, or helping make others happy. As a person matures, he or she will naturally gravitate toward doing something for which he or she has a calling. What may have been done out of duty in the beginning will give way to what needs to be done for fulfillment. And that may very well be an activity that is closer to the natural connectedness or intuitive knowing that is calling the individual from the higher Self. Once a person does whatever her calling is, or incorporates this new activity or lifestyle, she almost always finds that not only is she more inspired [in spirit], but will be an inspiration to others as well. You have no idea how many people are just waiting to be inspired, and you may be the one to provide the example for which they are waiting.

HAPPINESS FROM HELPING OTHERS

To channel your energy toward helping others is a sure way to inspire those around you. This is, in fact, a practical way for you to find happiness.

Especially in working to help the poor or those who are less fortunate than you. Helping others who are in need is a positive way to bring about your own happiness because such service is a genuine part of our spiritual nature.

There are many ways you can do this. You can directly work with those in need. Or you can donate the results of your work, either financially or with ready-made products, or with time given to worthy causes that improve the world and help others. And such beneficial acts will leave your mark, however insignificantly, for others' benefit. This is real fame. In whatever way you do this, you can not go wrong. Voluntary service to help others always brings happiness.

Such kindness is of three kinds. One kind is to show compassion to a person's material body through auspicious deeds, such as providing food to the hungry, giving water to the thirsty, medicine to the sick and clothes to the poor. Another type is to give knowledge to benefit one's mind and intellect. The third type is to show kindness for one's soul. This helps relieve a person from worldly suffering by giving him knowledge of his spiritual position and relationship to the Supreme. This actually surpasses all other levels of kindness. This is what is needed most because it can relieve all other forms of suffering.

In fact, it is explained in such ancient Vedic texts as the *Garuda Purana* that as one makes spiritual progress, if a person does not engage in kindness and compassion to others, one's life is merely superficial. Thus, such people distant themselves from finding true happiness. Such people prove themselves to be primarily interested in their own temporary pleasure of the mind and senses. Thus, they do not take the time to help others, or at least without their own interest in mind. If a person says he is trying to find true happiness yet does not make any attempt to assist others, he is far from understanding his spiritual identity and reaching his connectedness with his inner Self, which is also connected with all other beings. The fact is, we are all spiritual in essence, and on that level we are all equal and related to one another. If one is unhappy to see the distress of others and happy to see their legitimate happiness, he is on the right path toward spiritual understanding. Why? Because when one feels the happiness and distress of others as his own, that is the essence of the principle of real nonviolence and compassion, and practical spiritual vision. As it is further explained, if one has a body, which itself is temporary and may perish at any moment, and does not use it and its possessions and wealth to some degree for the benefit of others, then his body and all that belongs to it is considered to be merely a source of trouble.[1]

This brings us to our next point, that to be happy you must know how to use wealth properly.

USING WEALTH PROPERLY

The desire of most people is to acquire money. With money, so much can be done. It may be needed to buy food, pay rent, or take care of one's family. Yet, what most people want is to engage in less than virtuous activities. So how can money bring true happiness if it is used incorrectly, or for the wrong reasons? In such a case, it is better not to have too much money.

Though wealth may help bring an ease to life and freedom from certain problems, it is never the cause of real happiness. Even the wealthy have their share of anxiety and fear, sometimes more than those who are not so wealthy. Thus, real happiness is beyond all that. After all, as we look around we can plainly see that all men, no matter whether they be of high or low positions, experience great labor, fear, and anxiety in their attempt to attain, increase, protect, or enjoy their wealth. Even if a person who has grown up with easy money should ever lose his wealth, he will find that those who have become attached to him, such as brothers, wife and friends, may even break off their affectionate dealings or even abandon him. They may even squabble and become angry with him over small amounts of money. So we should ask, how much happiness can there be in such endeavors?[2]

One reason why this happens is that out of all that attracts a person in this material existence, wealth and riches bewilders one's intelligence more than anything else. It can become like an intoxicant. Even having a beautiful body or being born in an aristocratic family, or being greatly learned does not invoke the bewilderment and false pride that comes from having wealth. The biggest problem is that when one is not morally sound or spiritually motivated, he will use his wealth in wasteful ways, spending it not on altruistic or beneficial projects, but in enjoying intoxicants, women, gambling, and other frivolous activities. Thus, not only is one's wealth wasted, but also his life.[3]

From this point, a man may engage in violence, thievery, duplicity, enmity, and other malevolent activities because of his concern for protecting or acquiring more and more money.[4] Because of this kind of greed, even the famous and virtuous lose their credibility and good qualities.[5] So, actually, the wealth of such misers allows them no happiness. In fact, by accumulating money by questionable means, it is the cause of their own self-torment, although they may be so self-absorbed that it may be oblivious to them. In spite of his wealth and opulence, a rich man who is controlled by his mind and senses, greedy to attain more power and money, suffers from unnecessary labor, insomnia and fear for various reasons. They suffer anxiety and problems due to government laws, police, or the threat of thieves, enemies, cheating family members, and time itself.[6] Furthermore, when he dies, his nefarious activities and wasted lifestyle gives him nothing but a journey to hell. He may think he is enjoying now, but it is for naught.[7] This is obviously not the direction that anyone should go if they want real happiness.

Basically, there are two ways of using money--materially or spiritually. Money is naturally required. You cannot live without it, at least not in our present society. If one has enough money to maintain body and soul together, lives by an honest means without unnecessary efforts, and keeps his life honest and simple, he will find that happiness is not difficult to achieve. He has what he needs and time to enjoy life, too. Furthermore, if such a person can also use a portion of his or her money for spiritual purposes, or to help alleviate the problems of others, that will make one's life even more complete. Otherwise, it is said that money will simply become a burden that pays the way to a lower existence in the future.[8] However, if a person is spiritually oriented and knows how to use money for the spiritual benefit of him or herself and others, then there is no amount of money that is too great. Yet, such a person is rare. Even those with the best of intentions can be inappropriately swayed when too much wealth is accumulated.

Therefore, it is advised that a person should divide his or her money into five parts--one part for their religion and spiritual growth, one part for their own good character, one part for material necessities, one part for enjoyment, and one part for maintaining family.[9] According to preferences, these may be divided in different ratios. If one has few needs, or a small family, then larger portions can be used for spiritual pursuits or helping others. By this means, a person can be happy in this world and in the next.

If one is born in an especially auspicious and materially opulent situation, such as in an aristocratic family, or with wealth, beauty, etc., but is not proud, and uses his or her life and wealth properly, that person is considered to be favored by God. Because he realizes that all he has are the gifts of God, he uses his possessions in the service of the Supreme and for the spiritual well-being of all. Such a person is never disturbed even while surrounded by great opulence. However, if such a person becomes arrogant over his possessions and property, and uses his money with selfish intent, then he will join the ranks of those heading downward as described in the few previous paragraphs.[10] One must know how to use money in the right way if he or she wants real happiness, and not merely for the easy and temporary stimulations that money can buy. For these often merely pave the way for distress, anxiety and future problems.

HAPPINESS IN KNOWING YOUR SELF

On the most elementary basis, you must know yourself: You must know what you want, what you need, what you desire, what you love, and what you are stuck with and what you can change. Some of these may be more practical than others. I mean you may want and desire to live in a multimillion dollar mansion, but you may have to settle for less. Besides, you must decide how that would benefit you. A multi-storey mansion may be too big, require too much labor, cleaning, and expenditures than a smaller house. So you need to work with what is most reasonable. Change what you can if you feel you must change anything, and accept your limitations and work with them rather than try to avoid or hide them. In other words, do not make things difficult for yourself by unnecessarily trying to be more than you are, or have more than you need. Be practical, and then grow and develop at your own pace. Nonetheless, do not remain stuck with what you feel you can outgrow, or stay with something that you no longer need. What you feel is holding you back may be nothing more than life requiring you to develop the means which will catapult you to higher potentials, and closer to your spirituality and inner connectedness with God, rather than leaving you stifled by restrictions. Once you get more connected with your higher Self, you will realize that you, or your mind, are your own worst limiting force. The real spiritual you is beyond material limitations. If you think otherwise, it means that you simply have not yet discovered your true, dynamic potential.

To put it another way, life may force you to get out of your comfort zone, or out of the box, so to speak, in order for you to test your limitless nature. Most people can only do this to a certain degree in any one lifetime. But do not hold yourself back when it comes to discovering your real spiritual identity. Once you do, it is a whole different world. You may be ready for it, or maybe not. Do not worry, it is not scary. You are not limited by age, race, sex, your physical condition, your mental or educational abilities, or whatever. But once you enter that doorway of truly recognizing your spiritual Self, the possibilities are endless. You never knew you had so many beautiful facets of your Self. You cannot even fathom them all. Nonetheless, that is where you want to be. I will explain more as we proceed through this book.

Following a spiritual path to perceive our higher Self is one of the most unique adventures life has to offer. On this quest one can understand that there is a divine order to things--everything is happening for a reason. What may be reversals in life now may be only preparations for the better things yet to come, which may not manifest unless you were to experience whatever trials are happening now. When you look at life as a spiritual unfolding, then everything in life has a reason, a purpose. And that purpose is for your ultimate good, your ultimate development. Or it is to help you find your full potential, at least if you do not miss the message. In that light, no matter what happens, you are always getting better, wiser, higher, and closer to who and what you really are.

In the meantime, God and the spiritual energy that originates from Him is always supporting you. You simply need to be open to it and let it in to help you with any difficulties. With this point of view, even difficult times become easy. Unfortunately, if you are too egotistical, if you try to be too self-indulgent, too in control, you can miss it. You can fail to get the message. It is still there, but you will miss the opportunity to accept the support that is coming from God. Every situation gives us an opportunity to make it the most we can, to make ourselves the best we can.

In attaining happiness by knowing your Self, you may also begin to recognize that such feelings as sadness, disappointment, fear, anger, guilt, etc., are all temporary states of mind, and are minor obstacles. There may be so many reasons for such feelings, but do not listen to them too much. And even though they must be acknowledged and dealt with, you still need to rise above these to reach a state of constant happiness, or the state of tranquility and spirituality. If the mind is too busy telling you what it wants and what you should do and how you should feel, you cannot be receptive to inner guidance, or hear the voice of God, so to speak. Absorbed in your adverse feelings, you may think that life is unfair and that no one cares for you, not even God. Your mind may create a whirlpool of downward emotions, and you may be so convinced that everything you are thinking is absolutely correct. But how is God supposed to cut through all that interference without taking some drastic measures that may force you to sit down, take a look around, and reevaluate things? Such lessons may be required to learn points the hard way. This is why many yogis and spiritual teachers explain how we need to rise above the dictates of the mind, or quiet the mind, in order to connect with the soul, our real identity, which is beyond the body and mental platform. This is important to help perceive who we really are, and what we really are meant to do with ourselves and our real position in the universe. Only by understanding this can you make a connection with the Complete Beingness of the creation, and connect with your true destiny. Then you can know your purpose for being here and be truly happy and feel fulfilled in what you do in life. We must remember that spiritual growth is primarily an internal journey, but our progress can manifest externally in so many ways. And one of those ways is to invoke peace and happiness into our lives from within, regardless of our present situation.

So another key point is to learn your soul's purpose and then follow your destiny. This destiny is like flowing with the river of life which will take you where you need to be at the right time, and when you need to be there, even though there will be challenges. Things that come easy often do not give as much happiness nor provide the means to develop ourselves as something that requires a challenge. Remember, anything requires a little austerity or self-sacrifice, no matter whether it is starting your own business, raising a family, or even getting connected to your soul or going to heaven. Do not be afraid of the hardships. Actually, they are only lessons trying to show us something within ourselves that we have not gotten right yet. Now is our chance to get it right.

So in spite of whatever difficulties we go through, we can rise above it. That is our challenge, or our life's lesson. Do not fail the classroom by begrudging it, no matter what it may be, only to have a similar test later on. The challenge is our experience, it is not our identity. *We have to begin to separate our identity from whatever may be happening around us.* They are two different things. We are still able to be independently happy if we want to be.

Actually, why shouldn't the world be a difficult place? It is meant to give us the lessons for us to get closer to learning what we really are, until we eventually find out. The world is not our real home, and the only reason why life may seem challenging is that we want so many things that the world actually does not provide, or it provides them for only temporary lengths of time. For example, do not look for security in a world that offers only insecurity through constant change. This is common sense. The world, and everything in it, is always changing. All great sages, wise men and scripture will tell you to be detached from the temporary. Why do you think they are teaching you that? Because you cannot be happy while being attached, or identifying with, that which constantly changes through ups and downs, life and death, beginnings and endings. This duality is foreign to our spiritual nature, which makes it obvious that we will never be truly happy while trying to make arrangements for it within this temporary world. It just does not work. Sure, we can be happy in between the problems and tribulations. That is what so many are forced to contend with, feeling whatever temporary relief there may be between problems, until they again are dealing with dilemmas while hoping things will improve. But who wants to downgrade to that if there is something better? Believe me, you have no idea how much better it can be until you have personally perceived your own spiritual nature. That is when the fireworks go off. Then you will wonder, "Why didn't I ever see things this way before? What has been wrong with me? Old too soon, smart too late." Well, folks, we do not want to get stuck in these limitations. And how to be free of that is what we are revealing.

HAPPINESS IN LOVE

This is another kind of happiness, being in love with someone, which is essential for most people. Do you ever notice that when people are in love with someone special, who reciprocates their love, they seem to be in a better mood, like they love the whole world? In our search for happiness, a major motivational factor is that we all want to love and be loved. Loving is a natural state, a part of the eternal nature of the soul. However, while thinking we are this body, we often look for love through bodily affection. Thus, we try to be happy by attempting to satisfy the body or mind by finding someone who will give us the affection we desire. We figure once we find that other person, then everything will be great.

One thing we need to understand in our search for happiness is that you don't need someone else to make you complete. The key is to know that you already are a complete person. Do not depend on others for your self-esteem and happiness. You do not need to expect that from outside yourself. But, of course, you can let someone you love add to the joy and happiness you already have. Nothing wrong with that. But, if you do not have it on your own, do not think that merely by having another person will fill the emptiness. That is expecting too much, especially if the person you are with is desiring the same thing from you. Such a partnership or marriage will never last. Have you ever noticed that just as relationships between people can be a source of happiness, most of the problems that people have come from relationships?

The point is that your life and happiness do not actually depend on anyone else. This sort of happiness that is dependent on others is based on the illusion that you are your body and you are not complete without another body to keep you company. If you are not happy with yourself, you cannot be happy just by being with another man or woman, that is because your real identity is not being half a person, waiting for the other half to show up.

Some people have been waiting a long time, and they still have not found that special person. Or they thought they did find the right person only to learn they made a big mistake. So they are still waiting and still searching for happiness, thinking that it is still outside of them. But no, you have to be happy with yourself before you can be truly happy with anyone else. Then when you are happy with yourself, you will be much more selective about who are your friends and who you are with. And you will be much happier and fulfilled just by being with yourself. Then if you do meet someone special, the joy, love and happiness between the two of you will be much more fulfilling and mature. You will be a complete person meeting another complete person. What does that mean? It means there will be two, that's right, two complete persons coming together, instead of two halves of a whole, even though some people like to say it that way because it sounds romantic or something. To me it sounds more problematic. It means without one the other is not complete. Right? Now who wants that? If I want to be with someone, I do not want them to be half a person. Then you will be trying to figuring out which half you want, top or bottom, right or left... No, I'll take a whole person please. I think that would be more fun anyway. Ok, ok, I will get serious again.

Yes, the ultimate happiness is to love and be loved, but higher than a personal relationship is the love for the universe, or God, and knowing that all things and all entities are a part of that. In this way, your universal love encompasses all beings and all parts of God. All other kinds of love are merely leading up to that, or are instruments that direct us toward that kind of all-inclusive and spiritual love.

We are all looking to give our love, to give our Selves, to an all-loving person. But such a lover, such a fulfilling and never-ending relationship can only be found on the spiritual level of existence. Everything else, all other relations come and go, or end with death, bound by the restrictions found in bodily relations. However, Truth is the divine and eternal knowledge of the soul. All relations that are based on this Truth are also eternal, though the form of the relationship may change. Thus, as we become closer to truly understanding our higher Selves, we are all the wiser not to compromise our relations to anything less than that which is spiritual. Or at least we can gradually raise whatever we have to the spiritual level. In that state of being, all of our relations take on new meaning and reach a higher purpose, a higher sense of stability, wherein there is also a higher state of happiness.

That ultimate state of loving happiness can only be attained within a relationship centered on the Complete, the Complete Person, the Supreme Being. Once our relations are centered in that direction, there will be no other love that can compare. It is, indeed, the happiness for which we are always seeking.

□

5
How Our Consciousness Determines What We Want for Happiness

In understanding how to be truly happy in this material world, we should take a look at how our thoughts and needs change as we grow from childhood to adult, and how our thinking and consciousness will determine what will make us happy. These will provide a clue to the usual pattern of concerns and forms of happiness for which we look as we grow or go through the various stages of life.

The numerous concerns that affect the individual and how he or she views what is needed for happiness are divided into stages that in Sanskrit are called *annamaya*, *pranamaya*, *manomaya*, *vijnanamaya*, and *anandamaya*. I will analyze these one at a time. First there is *annamaya*, wherein, since *anna* means food, the individual is food conscious. In other words, when one is a baby and first growing up, one's main concern and source of happiness is in getting enough food. In this level of consciousness, when one has food in the stomach or can eat sumptuously, he is no longer anxious but is happy. So, when one is in *annamaya*, his goal is to get nice food. Then he is comfortable. Everyone is affected by this form of happiness to some degree. However, for one who remains on this level, his biggest source of happiness is eating.

The next level of concern and stage of life one goes through is described as *pranamaya*, the consciousness of being alive or continuing one's existence. In this level of consciousness, if a living being can live without being attacked or killed he thinks he is happy. Therefore, when affected by *pranamaya*, a living being will work hard in order to defend or protect himself from enemies or attackers, or other problems. For as long as he is successful in this way, he feels happy.

We can see these two levels of consciousness all around us. For example, as we look at a newborn baby, it cries whenever it is in pain or hungry. If it is fed nicely and given a place where it feels comfortable, it will rest in peace. So its first longings for happiness is to be fed and to feel safe and secure. So, this is how it is absorbed in *annamaya* and *pranamaya*.

Animals are much the same. Animals that live in the forest have little knowledge of anything but their hunger and thirst. Their instinct is based on the need to survive, which is to find food and avoid enemies. They have little perception of anything else. This is why those who are grossly materialistic are sometimes compared to animals. The reason is explained that such people think that economic development is the most important aspect of life because what they want more than anything is plenty of food and protection, at any cost, even at the expense of killing other living beings to eat them, just like many animals do. Or they may surround themselves with firearms, guns, fences, or other means to keep intruders and enemies away. And they may take great pride in their guns or weapons. This *annamaya* and *pranamaya* is their level of happiness.

The next stage is called *manomaya*. *Mano* means mind, so this is the platform of trying to make the mind content with various forms of pleasure, usually taken in through the five senses. When the mind is occupied with some sensual stimuli, thrills, or entertainment, the individual feels happy. This may also include the use of drugs or intoxicants to stimulate or even deaden the mind. For some people the mind is too active. They want to calm it or simply forget about everything that bothers them. They want to get away from their problems by visiting the river of forgetfulness through intoxication. Often this form of happiness on the *manomaya* platform, whether by thrills and chills, or the use of drugs, is especially fleeting because such happiness usually exists only between two problems. While one forgets his problems, there may be some happiness. However, it is often not long before another concern enters the picture. You know, like, "OK, the fun is over. Now back to reality." That kind of thing.

As you look around, you can see that most humans exist within these three levels of consciousness, *annamaya*, *pranamaya*, and *manomaya*. If they have not progressed much more than this, then these are the types of happiness for which they will be searching. And after attaining them, they think this is all they need. So they will be fairly satisfied with eating, sleeping, mating and defending. For example, it is said that if you want to tame a lion, make sure it is well fed. If it is too hungry, it will not be thinking about learning or carrying out any new instructions. It will only be looking at the trainer as an item on the menu. In many ways, it is the same way with people. If they are undernourished for happiness, so to speak, they will be looking at things around them wondering if or how it might be something that can provide them with pleasure. This may include food, drugs, big houses, pretty girls or handsome men, and so on. They are simply looking and thinking of how they can get pleasure or happiness from things that they desire. On the other hand, if they are well fed, have a place for protection, and something to keep them busy and occupied from thinking too much about the wrong things, like say disease and death, they will be happy. And that is where many people are at. Well, not all people. Some need a little more than that, which brings us to the next level.

The next stage, at least for humans, is *vijnanamaya*, the level of establishing one's philosophical values and self-identity. If a person can figure out what he wants to do, and where he fits into life, and then arrange one's values so that they suit him, he may feel justified in whatever his situation or actions may be. They may or may not make sense to others. Yet, in his philosophical rambling he justifies it to himself.

In this stage, in order to help himself make sense of things, a person may simply adopt the teachings of those who are considered creditable and to provide himself with a path to follow. This may be recognized by one's acceptance of a certain religion, or using a type of psychotherapy or analysis, or following a particular political leader, or even adapting the same looks and views of a popular artist or musician, or so on. Thus, one picks or figures out an identity and a purpose in life, a reason for doing something. And this is the type of happiness for which one searches in the *vijnanamaya* stage.

When a person has this sorted out, then he or she feels happy. Of course, if someone challenges his assorted values, philosophy or religion, then he may feel he has to defend himself. If his ego is too big, and his identity with a certain sect or outlook is quite rigid, and this is being challenged, trouble begins. It is because if he or his set of values are defeated, he may feel that he loses his sense of identity and purpose. Then what will he do? So he gets defensive to keep from feeling this confusion. This again hinges on the *pranamaya* level of consciousness wherein one feels happy if he can defend himself and be victorious for his own sense of purpose and well being. This happens all the time.

Have you ever been around two people who fanatically hold their own values but challenge those of others, or who criticize anyone who is different? It is not always pretty. That is why it is sometimes said that you should not talk about religion or politics with others if you want to avoid controversy or quarrel. On the other hand, another person may simply rearrange his values in order to adjust to the new information and outlooks that make more sense.

Vijnanamaya is also the level in which exists the process of "becoming," or reaching the point of who you think you are and what your values will be. So this platform offers a level of happiness that can also change with time or with new forms of understanding.

So, most people exist primarily on these four platforms of consciousness, which may all interchange due to varying levels of priority from time to time. This means that for the majority of people, as long as they can acquire nice food by economic development, have their life protected by nice house or clothes or defense mechanisms, have various forms of entertainment and recreation, or be surrounded by family and friends, and establish their own philosophical values which may include religious or political preferences, then they may feel that life is good and will be quite content. Therefore, as you can see, this is what most people pursue in their attempts to find happiness. They think this is the main purpose of life. And because of the search, or I should say the hope, to attain this kind of happiness, a person will undergo so many difficulties. They may base their career on the design that once they can make enough money, all of these previously mentioned items will have a chance of falling into place. If they do, then everything is great. Yet, often what happens is that a person may get one or two things sorted out, and still remain waiting for everything else to appear in his life. They think, "If I only had this." Or, "If things were only like that, then everything would be fine." Thus, the hope for complete happiness continues, as it should, but it needs to be focused in the right direction.

The point is that while a person exists on the level of consciousness in which he is absorbed in *annamaya*, *pranamaya*, *manomaya*, and *vijnanamaya*, he or she may be happy with the basest of things in life, but their ideal state of full contentment and happiness remains out of reach. And they may not even know why. It is just like grabbing for the ring while riding the merry-go-round. Each time you go around you reach for that ring. If you do not get it the first time, you want to try for it the next time. Or like the donkey and the carrot. You get the donkey to move by holding a carrot on a stick in front of him. The donkey keeps trying to reach the carrot, but just cannot quite seem to reach it. It is always just a little further ahead of him. Then he thinks that if he could only go a little further he would get it, but never does.

Likewise, our anticipation for complete fulfillment keeps us moving forward in hopes that we will reach a level of real happiness. The problem is that it does not really exist in these levels of consciousness. The happiness that can be found in these stages of development are all temporary and subject to change. And change they do. Therefore, this is the reason why life can be like a juggling act to keep everything together in order to be happy and have a chance at complete fulfillment. In other words, there is no real substance here. You may need food, house and home, wife or husband, family, entertainment, and philosophical adjustments on the material platform to maintain the body and mind. And you certainly may have that and be proud of it. But this has little to do with the soul, your real Self. Only on that stage, and acting with those things in life that relate to your real Self, can there be any tangible forms of happiness that are not so fleeting, like food, money, position, status, family, sex, entertainment, intoxication, or whatever else it takes that you think you need. That is not real happiness. In fact, too much of any one of those can get you into trouble. Therefore, happiness is within. Yet, you have to know how to reach that inner state.

It is because of ignorance that the living being accepts the material body as his real identity, and, thus, pursues whatever means possible to try to please himself through bodily and mental happiness. He accepts nonpermanent objects and activities as the means by which happiness can be found. Furthermore, the body itself often becomes a source of trouble. Just by having one, a person is subject to the pains and problems that the body may cause. Because of the material body, a person must also accept the pains and pleasures that are created by others, or by nature. For example, on some days the weather may be beautiful, yet the winter can bring terrible cold, blowing snow, and conditions that make life difficult. Those around you can also be friends and give some happiness, while others may create all kinds of problems for you, like the gossips that spread nasty rumors about you, or insects that want to bite, dogs that bark all night keeping you from sleeping, and so on. This is life? You better believe it, as long as you have this body. Of course, this physical apparatus is an amazing machine. After all, it is a part of you that allows you to express yourself in this world. But it is also different from your spiritual identity. Due to not perceiving or understanding this point is the reason why the common man desires to find happiness through the process of satisfying the mind and senses.

In illusion one thinks he or she can be happy by making various plans and arrangements for the body and mind, and its many attachments, such as house and family. Since these are all temporary, they can only give a limited amount of pleasure. And the attempt to make such orchestrations often merely entangles one deeper in responsibilities and complexities, and thus takes a person farther away from the happiness that one actually seeks. Therefore, it could be asked, do you own your possessions and means of happiness, or do they own you? Are you the one working so hard to maintain what you have? Do your desires and objects of pleasure force you to strain yourself with undesirable work? Of course, everyone has to maintain themselves in order to live. However, are you really doing what you want, or would you have more freedom if you simplified your life?

This is why a person may make so many arrangements and feel that they are quite content and satisfied, only to look at himself years later and realize he feels empty and unfulfilled, or even trapped by his situation. What first looked so sweet later turns to be only sour grapes. The reason is that the person still has not been able to truly understand his spiritual identity, or continues to try and squeeze pleasure out of his body or something that has little if anything to do with his real identity, his spiritual Self.

It is the nature of material life to be insecure. Like a man may find a woman he can love, but there is the threat that she may get tired of the situation and leave. Or another man may steal her away. Or she may make so many demands that she may not be worth the trouble anyway. Or even if the love is secure, how long can it last? Death may come and force separation. This is the continual risk that everyone takes in this material realm, and in seeking happiness through the endeavor of trying to satisfy the mind and senses. The truth is, the mind and senses can never be fully appeased. Such fulfillment does not exist in them because it is their job to tell you continually what they need and want. If one is not in control of his senses, the senses alone force one to spend so much money on new things in seeing, smelling, tasting, touching, hearing, and desiring. It is like being addicted to drugs; you spend so much until you have nothing left. Then you jeopardize your job and future. For the sake of temporary enjoyment, a person may risk everything. In such a case, he chases after the illusion of sensual happiness like a mirage in the desert. Because of this, a person seeking happiness becomes increasingly implicated in unhappiness, like someone seeking honey from a beehive and being stung by the bees.

So the more you identify with the body, the more you will be motivated to seek out newer and newer experiences, even if it is just more and more ice cream or chocolate, in order to have some satisfaction. It is like pouring gasoline on a fire. The more you feed it, the more it will consume. The more it wants. Now imagine if you have a family wherein all of your dependents want you to do the same for them. You will be so busy with everyone else's needs and desires that you will hardly have any time for yourself. Now that is what I call fun.

One key point to understand is that this world offers no permanent relationship with anything or anyone, not with our loved ones or even our own body, which must be given up one day.[1] Time very quickly takes away the life of one with uncontrolled senses because such a person may be so busy trying to satisfy his mind and senses, yet makes no genuine spiritual advancement, and thus no preparation for the next life.[2] Therefore, no one should simply waste away in householder life without making some advancement toward spiritual realization before being dragged away at the time of death.[3] Otherwise, such a person remains attached to material life and longs to maintain his relationships and his desires for material happiness and pleasure while being carried away by death. Thus, not knowing where he is going, he dies in great pain and grief, wishing he could continue living, while his life appears like a flash in time.[4] After so many years, or even lifetimes, of being forced through these kinds of difficulties, a person will begin to ask why he or she is not yet happy. Why is he not fulfilled and content? Is there something more to life than this? If a person begins to ask these kinds of questions, then at last he can reach the next level of consciousness.

Finally, beyond the previously mentioned levels of awareness, we reach *anandamaya*. This is most often reached by evolving through the *vijnanamaya* stage of developing one's philosophical or religious values and understanding. In *anandamaya* a person reaches the intellectual platform that allows one to genuinely understand his or her spiritual identity, that he is not the body but the spiritual living being within it. Then one begins to take the spiritual path and to add transcendental aspects to one's life. In this way, a person departs from the more materialistic ways of happiness and starts to incorporate those things and activities that will directly connect one with their inner Self and give one genuine spiritual bliss. Before one reaches this level, they are considered to be on the material platform of life. Happiness on the material strata is most fleeting and illusory. There is little substance to it. It always comes and goes. Even if you find something that gives you some level of enjoyment and lasts for many years, in the end it will fade away if it is on the material level. This is simply the nature of the material energy. And you wonder why you may sometimes feel empty or unfulfilled?

Once one actually reaches the *anandamaya* stage and embraces genuine spiritual practices into his life, he begins to purify the consciousness, and anxiety and unhappiness leave. The reason why is because he becomes free from the previously mentioned levels of consciousness, namely the *annamaya*, *pranamaya*, *manomaya*, and *vijnanamaya* stages. The type of happiness that was once so important, as found in these stages of life, now becomes increasingly less significant. Now, on this level, the only sadness one may feel is the sorrow that comes from seeing the distress of others, which is a form of compassion. Such compassion is natural and spontaneous for one who is on the path of spiritual progress. It is also necessary for one who wants to continue their spiritual development. Then one can truly feel the pain of others and begin working to help all living beings on a spiritual level.

It is in this stage that one can begin to realize that happiness cannot be achieved merely by working hard for sensual or mental thrills. Everyone knows that the chief aim of life is to try to rid themselves of miseries and sources of anxiety. Nonetheless, this is impossible by surrounding ourselves with pleasures and comforts for which we must work hard to attain, or for which we need to engage in questionable activities. Such objects later become only sources of attachment or even confinement to the material platform of life. It coerces us into continuing our enslavement in the service of the temporary mind and senses.[5] Thus, we are forced to continue within the cycles of duality, consisting of varying degrees of happiness and distress, ups and downs, birth and death, or favors and curses from those around us. These are in themselves natural by-products of our contact with this material existence.[6] In other words, regardless of one's position in this world, a person will automatically experience happiness or unhappiness.[7] It cannot be avoided. Even if one has the luxury of being financially independent, he may be merely working off whatever good he has coming to him in this life. Yet he cannot completely control what he needs to be happy, for in this world happiness and distress follow each other like the seasons. Why? Because it is based on the material energy, which itself is constantly changing from nice and pleasant to annoying or even miserable. In this way, as you identify with your surroundings, your disposition changes, regardless of what kind of material facility you may have, such as lots of money, big house, plenty of food and drink, and whatever else you can imagine. Then it all becomes monotonous after enough time goes by. Why? Because it does not touch the real you, the spiritual

Self, which is merely waiting dormantly for you to attend to your real needs, which are spiritual.

The main goals of materialistic life are to eat, sleep, sex, attain economic success, and add as much luxury as one can fit into one's existence, along with the piety of religion, at least in most cases, and assisting others to some degree. These may all be necessary to an extent, yet these are all primarily based on the identity of the temporary material body, and are thus inconsequential to the spiritual being that exists within. The body is like a container in which we live, like being surrounded by a bag through which we see, hear, taste, smell, and feel. But it is not our real Self. As we begin to understand this, we can perceive the fact that the happiness and distress which is based on one's bodily contact with the material energy are mistaken ideas.[8] They exist in the lower levels of consciousness, such as *annamaya*, *pranamaya*, *manomaya*, and even *vijnanamaya*. Yet, on the *anandamaya* platform, one can begin to see how everything that is happening within the world of time is merely like a dream.[9] First, it is all subject to the nebulous interpretations of the mind and senses, regarding whether the experiences are accepted as good or bad, plus, they are all temporary with constant changes of beginnings and endings. And we have all been told by the great sages and deliverers of the world, such as Buddha, Jesus, Mohammed, Krishna, and many others, not to be attached to the temporary, and to find real happiness only in that which does not change. However, even a child of eight may know this, but hardly a man of eighty can put it into real practice. This is the difference between those of the *annamaya*, *pranamaya*, *manomaya*, and *vijnanamaya* levels of consciousness, and those who have reached the *anandamaya* stage.

The mental platform is most flickering, and the attractions for happiness on that level change with every moment that goes by. In other words, the mind wants one thing at one minute, then something else the next. So, those who exist on the lower levels of consciousness have many kinds of demands for what they want in order to be happy. Yet we can see that it often changes from hour to hour, and from person to person, and it never stays the same for long. Therefore, we must again state that happiness and distress, when based on one's bodily and mental conceptions, and one's contact with the material energy, are mistaken ideas. In other words, they are not truly related to our ultimate and superior identity as spiritual beings.

Maybe no one has ever come right out and told you this before, or maybe you had this thought, but never quite expressed it this way. Yet, joy and sorrow are only due to one's perception of what goes on around him. That depends on how the pleasant or disagreeable sensations are interpreted by the mind, and whatever our mental disposition happens to be at the moment. Because of this, different people will have varying opinions about the same situation or experience. This is also the basis of how we think we are happy or not. It is, for the most part, an interpretation of the ever-changing conditions that go on in the material world that are a natural occurrence. Someone may love winter and its deep white snows, and someone else may hate it. It is all a matter of personal interpretation as situations are sifted through the mind that judges whether things are agreeable or disagreeable. Therefore, we can again reiterate that happiness and distress in the material world of duality are simply mental judgements and concoctions based on sensual and mental contact with the things around us.

In this way, we can understand how genuine happiness cannot be attained merely by so much plan-making or arrangements. Though they can certainly help in particular ways, nonetheless we may make a plan to build a house for our happiness, but if that house burns down for some reason, that same house becomes a source of our distress. This is the nature of material happiness. Thus, by increasing our plans to enjoy our mind and senses through various activities does not guarantee happiness. It often leads to the path of anticipation for happiness in the hope that we will acquire it soon. However, we often find that we are continually working hard simply to deflect or resolve the problems that constantly present themselves. As I have said before, that is not happiness.[10]

On the *anandamaya* stage, the world is filled with genuine happiness, because only on the *anandamaya* platform can one begin to connect with the real Self, and rise above the mental dictations of what is agreeable and disagreeable as interpreted through the temporary mind and senses. Even when getting a glimpse of the *anandamaya* stage, or when we link our real identity to our spiritual being, one's perception of the world and the Self begins to change, what to speak of when one fully enters it. On this platform, one can rise above and never feel the problems that exist in the world of duality, at least not as we had before. Therefore, we can also see that the world is full of happiness. Yet, we need to reach that genuine level of spiritual substance wherein real happiness exists. That is why when we feel unfulfilled with our lives, it is a natural sign telling us that we need to add some real substance in order to be connected to our higher Self, and to feel the fulfillment and contentment for which we are always looking. That is a secret that you will learn, how to put that substance in your life.

Ultimately, life is an adventure to improve yourself in every way, up to the point of realizing your true spiritual Self or identity. Thus, life is like a classroom with lessons that allow you to advance and learn more about yourself and spiritual Truth. The lessons can be a smooth flow of progress or a difficult transition, the latter of which is due to your reluctance to let go and be malleable to what the universe, fate, destiny, or God wants you to do and learn. Just like school, if you fail the grade, you simply keep going through the same class until you finally pass the test. Yet that is the great thing about spiritual progress: You simply keep going until you make the grade, in how many ever years or lifetimes it takes. No one really fails, some just take it slower or need more time than others.

□

6

What Keeps Us From Being Truly Happy

What keeps us from being truly happy is quite simple really, yet difficult to put into practice until we really understand it. The fact of the matter is that the living entity is a pure spiritual being, but encased within a material body. What this means is that the individual soul, when in the materially conditioned state, identifies itself as this temporary body, which may, for example, be male or female, black or white, young or old, American or Russian, healthy or sickly, or something else. When our real identity, which is spiritual, is transferred to the temporary body, all of the desires that the living entity has are then focused on the physical form, centered around the mind and senses. So the living being then tries to seek pleasure and satisfaction by serving the mind and senses. The problem is that there is a lack of reality in material existence since its basis is on the wrong identity. Material activities have little to do with the spiritual being within the body. Therefore, at some point the living being, who is almost lying dormant in the material form, will become restless with this lack of attention for its spiritual needs and start to wake up to the fact that he is still not fulfilled or satisfied, in spite of how many material engagements have occupied him. This then carries over into material consciousness, and the person will then feel unhappy or incomplete with the way things have gone.

So it is the material mind and senses that have desires for sensual pleasure, which the mind may interpret as happiness. Yet the soul is still waiting for the proper attention to fulfill its own spiritual needs. The soul is simply the observer of material activities, and does not participate in them. It is like watching a movie, or having an out of body experience when merely watching what the body is doing, or what is happening to the body. But the soul is not the material body. It is only within it.[1] The correct understanding is that the gross physical and subtle bodies (consisting of mind, intelligence and false ego) have nothing to do with the pure spirit soul within the body. They are simply a superficial or subtle covering of the pure Self.[2] For this reason it is considered that the most foolish part of spiritual ignorance is identifying with the temporary material body. It is this misconception that precedes the idea that my legs, my hands, or my head are actually myself. Then all that appears to be connected with the body becomes "my" wife, "my" husband, "my" family, "my" property, "my" job or duties, "my" money, and on and on. All this continues without considering that we came into this world with nothing, and when we die we take with us nothing. Then everything in between those two conditions called birth and death are but temporary activities and belongings that do not really have much of a connection with our real identity as the spiritual being within the body.[3] This is what people forget to consider, and what gives rise to the numerous problems that follow this initial misconception.

The main foolishness of the gross materialistic lifestyle is that people work very hard for what they think will be a permanent home, family, or career. What upsets most people is when they learn or experience that nothing is permanent. Something always happens sooner or later to disrupt or take away what they have been working to accomplish or acquire.[4] So in truth, the spirit soul only "imagines" or "pretends" (for lack of better words) that he or she is the material body. Yes, the body is real, and so is a dream, but only as long as the person does not wake up from the dream. Once he awakes, then he sees through the illusion of the experience, regardless of how real it may have seemed to be. Similarly, as a person enjoys or suffers in a dream, life on the material plane is also illusory and full of joys and sorrows of short duration that have little to do with the spiritual Self. In this way, without proper regard for our spiritual identity, one thinks he is a permanent part of this temporary world.[5] The individual and independent soul is transcendental or above the material nature. It exists on a much higher frequency or vibrational level. Thus, the soul can never actually be affected by material happiness or distress. It is only due to the false or bodily ego that causes the physical covering to overwhelm the spiritual being and consider itself a material form. This further creates the tendency for one to enjoy or suffer while influenced by bodily activities, although a person is actually above it all. The purpose of spiritual practice is to relieve a person from this condition, and reawaken one to his or her genuine spiritual identity.

Therefore, once again, because there is no real or permanent connection between the living being and matter, all happiness and distress have no essential reality in material existence. They go on as regular events, with you or without you. The more we think we are these material bodies that need to be served and catered to, the more we will be absorbed in the illusory highs and lows of life, which have little to do with who and what we really are. *This is the main reason why our material engagements are limited in how much happiness or pleasure they can ever give us.*

ALL SUFFERING EXISTS ONLY WITHIN THE ILLUSION

This is a very important point to understand.

No matter what kind of suffering we may feel, whether it is hunger, the need for sleep, our anger, jealously, anxiety, fear of something, it is all based on identifying with our physical or mental well-being. It is all connected with bodily concerns.

If we were really and fully situated in the spiritual aspect of life, we would never feel any suffering. That does not mean that we would not be concerned for those who remain in the illusion of the temporary joys and sorrows of life. Naturally, compassion is one of the feelings of the soul, wanting to do good for others who are all parts of God. But for ourselves, once we are spiritually situated, we can see that happiness and distress in material life is built around mental confusion.[6] It is our material conditioning that makes us feel that one thing is good or pleasant, and something else is bad or unpleasant. Similarly, our creation of friends and enemies in this world is built on this same sort of mental interpretation and conditioning, like a dream wherein we create so many situations out of imagination or impressions from the subconscious.[7]

The fact is that we are all spiritual beings, sons and daughters of God. Yet, when we are all acting on the impulse that we are these material bodies which need to be satisfied according to the desires in the mind, it forces us to act in many different selfish ways which are then interpreted as being friendly to some and adverse to others. It is all like acting on the illusory stage of material life, each of us wearing a particular costume, yet whose real identity is far different than the part that we play. The spirit soul naturally exists in a unified state of pure consciousness. However, when appearing in this world and in a variety of physical forms, each soul can be overwhelmed and mistaken regarding the purpose of life and our real identity. Thus begins the false conception of life.

Because the material world is an illusion of flickering commodities that are "Here today, gone tomorrow," our numerous attachments tend to be the cause of our anxiety. For example, in thinking that our mortal body is our real self, we become attached to what gives any little pleasure or happiness. Thus, we become attached to our spouses, children, wealth, house, property, or our career. And by trying to hold on to them and keep life balanced so that we can protect all that we have and see that everything flows smoothly, these very attachments put us in a position which creates most of our worry and concern.[8]

In this way, we may begin to see that our position in this world, being a misidentification of what we really are, for the most part, is full of fear.[9] Not only do we want to maintain what we have, but we must also continue to provide for ourselves and our dependents. We must work for our food, our shelter, clothes, our health, our means of transportation, our protection, and so on. Plus, the problem of finding a perfect mate seems to be an ongoing concern for most people. What if a person cannot find someone? Will he or she have to live alone? What if she finds someone and he is not what she was hoping for? Then will she have to start all over again? This just goes on and on, for both men and women. When does it end? Or sometimes even if things are going well, we become afraid of what kind of problem might happen next. Have you ever noticed how some people say that when things are going too well, something bad is going to happen? Or we simply may be afraid of whatever changes the future might bring. We may feel fear of being homeless, or unemployed, or dumped by our spouse, and worry about the safety of our children, or about death. Therefore, in many ways, the happiness we perceive is merely the forgetfulness of the constant problems that this world presents. However, all of these problems exist only within the illusion that we are these temporary bodies. From that misconception comes all of this fear and the sources of anxiety.

Outside of this illusion, within the real understanding of who and what we are, there is no fear, no suffering, no anxiety, and no wrong choices. That is why, as it is explained in *Bhagavad-gita* (5.22), a wise person on the spiritual path, or one who knows his real spiritual identity, does not rely on the sources of happiness that come through contact with the material senses because they all have a beginning and an end. When you depend too much on such forms of happiness, such kinds of pleasure can also become sources of misery or disappointment when they are gone. This is another example of how all suffering exists only within the illusion.

Real Truth is not material nor temporary. It is the eternal knowledge of the soul and the one Supreme Soul. Bringing this information into one's life is the way by which we can mitigate the misconceptions we have about ourselves, and bring us out of the illusion and into that strata of never-ending happiness. Then we can really begin to help others and know what is best to do and how to be happy.

THE WRONG AIM OF LIFE

Because of the bodily conception of our identity, it brings us to the wrong aim of life, which is our motivation toward selfish material enjoyment. This is what keeps us in the illusion and prolongs whatever suffering and anxiety we may be experiencing. For example, when we have worked hard in our life and have struggled to attain a house, and are surrounded by wife or husband, children, community, have an education, a career, or whatever else we have wanted, sometimes we feel very happy. Sometimes we are completely jubilant, yet sometimes we are not so satisfied. At other times we may feel completely bewildered, not sure of what we want or what to do. In this way, for whatever reason, things are always changing. Again we find that what we think gives us security or happiness is an illusion because the mood of the mind is always fluctuating. Because of that alone, what once was like nectar in the beginning can become like poison in the end. When something is new it may be exciting, but after some time it can get dry and tasteless. That is the nature of the material world. So if you are looking for steady and sure happiness by being absorbed in the material energy, you must be aware of this shortcoming.

One key point here is that real happiness can be found in any condition, as long as you begin to make the connection with your higher Self. Once you realize that you are a spiritual being, you can understand that you are never connected to matter because you are a part of the superior spiritual energy of God. Always. You are a minute particle of eternity, bliss and omniscience. However, you are part of the marginal potency in the sense that you have the free will to either become absorbed in the material energy or be released from it. It is your decision. Once you make that decision, then you can engage in those practices to raise yourself, your consciousness, to higher levels of perception and attain freedom from the encroaching material problems that can, at times, seem overwhelming. Or you can remain absorbed in trying to relish whatever attracts your senses, and endure the ups and downs that go with it.

It is similar to the way a monkey is caught. He sees a nice piece of fruit in a jar and grabs for it, holding it in his hand. But the neck of the jar is too small for him to pull the fruit out, so he is caught with his hand in the jar, not knowing that if he simply let go of the fruit in his hand, he could immediately be released from the jar.

In the same way, when the mind is motivated by passion and attachments, a person is forced into making many plans. Then he pursues them and voluntarily accepts so many troubles in hopes of attaining happiness and something meaningful in this world as a result of his schemes. Through this means he expects to enjoy life. He sees a beautiful house, and he wants one. He sees a fast car, and he wants one. He sees a lovely lady, and he wants her. This is because he thinks that surrounding himself with such possessions will make him happy. He thinks that once he achieves any of these, then he can relish his accomplishments.[10] This is the way that achieving the results of one's hard work gives a false sense of happiness.[11] A person may feel that he has attained his goals, but such happiness soon gives way to the next desire or goal, or even the next problem. The fact of the matter is that one who cannot control his senses comes under the control of never-ending material desires. One with uncontrolled senses never feels satisfied with what he has for long. He always wants more or something new.[12] Thus, without realizing it, he is forced to act on those desires for more and more prizes, accomplishments, and possessions. His life often becomes more complicated, and the happiness he longs for keeps alluding him, like the donkey chasing after the carrot that is actually dangling from a string that is hanging from a stick that is fastened to the donkey's back. The donkey does not understand that the more he chases after the carrot, the more he is merely serving a master. This is merely the master's way of getting the donkey to do something with the promise of a reward. In the same way, the materialist is forced to continue to serve his unquenchable thirst for material enjoyment at the dictates of the master, known as his mind and senses.

Yet, as time goes on, he may question the course of action he has taken. He may indeed look around and wonder why he has not attained the happiness for which he had hoped. He sees that time has slipped away. In fact, he may be an old man, and if he has not kept himself so busy that he has no time to reflect on life, he may start to worry that death is drawing near. His friends may start to die off, giving a warning sign that his turn may be next. At that time, he may feel that all of his prizes, possessions, property, and wealth, have lost the meaning that they once had. They cannot protect him from death, and he has made no spiritual progress to console himself of what future lies ahead of him. Without proper spiritual knowledge, a person is left with nothing but his own ignorance for his counsel in trying to figure what to do. Thus, at death, the materialist is taken away from everything he had worked for and everything that had given him any pleasure, and another life goes by without gaining any substantial understanding of the true purpose of it.

WRONG AMBITIONS AND THEIR HIDDEN RESULTS

As we can see from the above description, and by looking around and noticing the general pattern in which most people are engrossed, those people who are trapped by the desire to enjoy material life cannot understand the real goal of earthly existence. One who is overly attached to the objects of material happiness cannot understand that he is wasting precious time by working to merely maintain house and home, or satisfy mind and senses.

The real purpose of life is to realize the Absolute Truth, and that chance is spoiled by the pursuit of too many materialistic goals. A foolish person cannot understand that life offers the chance for real liberation, freedom from the limitations that capture a person while in this material creation, and freedom from the essential problems of life, starting with birth, disease, old age and death.[13]

Unfortunate as it may be, those interested in enjoying a so-called beautiful life, surrounded by family and friends, and searching after wealth, think that such things are life's ultimate goal. Such people never find life's true purpose. Thus, they are forced to go through many lifetimes engaged in the same pursuits.[14] In this way, the conditioned soul continues to wander throughout the world in various lives searching after the same happiness as always. Sometimes he may be fortunate in a high position, and at other times he may suffer in a low circumstance. In any case, in his search for material happiness he is ever neglecting the way toward real freedom from these continuous ups and downs.[15]

As we all know, while living in the material world, we do need to make a living, and have money and necessities to survive and take care of the bodies in which we live. Nonetheless, a spiritually progressive person is not so interested in anything that is temporary. When he or she knows the transcendental pleasures of spiritual life, such a person will engage in the spiritual pursuits that deliver one to the unlimited happiness within the Absolute Truth, in connection with one's higher Self and the Supreme Being. After all, materialistic pleasures are available even to the hogs and dogs who also eat, sleep and have sex. What is the need for a human being to strive so hard for the same things? Better to strive for spiritual purification which allows our consciousness to enter into the spiritual strata wherein exists unlimited transcendental bliss. In such a state, the living being can attain self-sufficient happiness and feel that wherever he may be and at all times, without being dependent on temporary material facilities for sensual pleasure.

Therefore, the key point is that, yes, work to maintain yourself, keep your body and soul fit. Work to attain basic happiness while living in this world, but keep your life simple. This allows you to be free from the many complexities that actually create more problems and less peace of mind. Raise your family peacefully, if you have one. However, we should keep in mind that we must not be overly attached to anything without striving for spiritual consciousness. Such material attachment without the spiritual perspective is what leads us farther away from the true happiness and contentment that we seek.[16] We must reflect on how we can continue to aspire for keeping all of our relations in the proper frame work of spiritual Truth. That is where we all, not only ourselves but also the people with whom we are involved, can be truly happy and peaceful.

As it is questioned in the *Srimad-Bhagavatam* (3.13.50): "Who, other than one who is not a human being, can exist in this world and not be interested in the ultimate goal of life? Who can refuse the nectar of narrations about the Personality of Godhead's activities, which itself can deliver one from all material pangs?" This is the highest aim of life. Thus, it is clearly understood that only those in the lower stages of consciousness, such as the *annamaya*, *pranamaya*, and *manomaya*, and even the lower levels of *vijnanamaya*, would not be concerned about this ultimate purpose of human existence wherein is found the highest levels of happiness and pleasure.

□

7

Hey, Add Some Substance to Your Life, It's Time for a Change

As we learned in the last chapter, we are often absorbed in the wrong level of reality, or focused on that which exists outside of our real spiritual nature. So this is why when unexplained dissatisfaction occurs, much of the time it is simply because of the lack of reality and the superficial nature in material existence. You go around and around, so busy with so many things and in the end you still wonder if you have missed the point. Has the boat gone on without you? Are you still stuck hoping that things will change? Do you think that life has passed you by? Are you getting older and still wonder where is your place in the world? Or maybe the children have grown up and left home, leaving you and the house feeling empty. Or maybe you are still a young person trying to figure what the heck to do with your life, besides find a career and make lots of money? You want something that has meaning.

Before you continue with this chapter, make sure you have read or reviewed Chapter Four about starting to get connected to your higher Self. What is discussed there are the prominent forms of happiness. And beyond that, we need to understand, as introduced in the previous chapter, that material happiness for the spiritual being in this world is incompatible. It may work for a while, depending on one's level of consciousness. Yet, if one continues to evolve, a person is likely to find that what once provided him or her with pleasure has outgrown its usefulness or meaning. Thus, it does not give the same level of fulfillment as it once did.

Often times we can see that a big part of material happiness is merely whatever little pleasure one gets from counteracting sources of distress.[1] Mere lack of distress may be good enough for some people, but it is not real happiness, and at some point in the lives of many, they will begin to ask why they may be feeling empty and at a loss for fulfillment. This feeling is nothing more than the reasoning from your higher Self that you need to look elsewhere, inward for fulfillment, not to merely continue working for accomplishments and success on the material level. Such feelings mean that you are already discovering how there may be some comfort in material achievements, but real happiness that truly touches the core of who and what you really are exists on a higher level.

The first reason why people are often unfulfilled is that they may be stuck with things or situations that appears to be holding them back, back from whatever else they would rather be doing. Thus, the urge to escape is a dominant feeling in such circumstances. Escape to what, that is the next question. Sometimes people have a good idea what they would like to escape to, while others just want a change of situation. They do not always know what they want. But they do want to be free from what has become a stifling or stagnant circumstance. This is often what a person notices about themselves when they first begin to feel unfulfilled, no matter whether you are young or old.

This is not unusual in life. Why? Again because it is a voice from your higher Self giving the call. You have to understand that the needs of the soul will always be like a guiding voice, or a conscience asking whether you have all you want. Have you attained what you desire? Have you reached your goal? Have you acquired self-sufficient happiness? In all honesty, if you are simply serving your mind and senses, such a state of contentment is not possible for any long duration. There may be short periods of exhilaration. Or the thrill of the moment in a prize to be won, the heights to achieve, or the success to be had. These are great when they come, but they also surely go. And still, for many, they wonder what more is there. What's next?

The reason for this is that the first need of the soul is complete freedom. The real secret is to focus on the needs of the soul, your real identity. If a person is more than the body, then the only means of complete fulfillment is to reach that portion of the person which is higher than the mere physical machine in which one resides. And as long as you are in the material body, or identifying it to be your true identity, it is not easy to attain that state of complete freedom. It is like being in a row boat, and rowing furiously to get farther out into the lake, while not realizing that it is still anchored to the shore. In this way, there may be times when your Self gives you the beckoning, and you have the feeling that much of what you have done has contained so much useless labor, as if there has been little that has touched the real you. This is because the soul wants to be free from the limited realm of material bondage.[2] He even wants to be free from this entire universe, including the constraints of time and space. But complete freedom can be attained only when making the connection with the spiritual domain, with the one Complete Being, the Supreme Spirit. The soul will always hanker for that direction because it is the natural state of being for the soul, to serve and connect with the Supreme Soul. That is the purpose of religion and yoga. Its meaning is to unite, to unite the individual soul with the Supersoul. Therein lies the happiness for which we hanker. Therein we become truly connected with all that is, with our Higher Self, and with the divine nature which gives the ultimate freedom. No other state of being provides such bliss, ecstasy, or such unfathomable exhilaration.

Some of this may be new information to you, or seem foreign, or even sound silly. Yet, you have no idea how many lifetimes you have gone around this universe, always looking for happiness. You also have no idea how many more lifetimes you will keep going around if you continue to look anywhere else than the spiritual domain for the happiness that you seek. Therefore, now that we are in this human form of life, we should try to engage ourselves in the means by which we can evoke our own divine consciousness, and attain our own self-sufficient happiness. We need to take up engagements that give us liberation to the region beyond this material confinement, wherein there is complete freedom. That state can be attained right now, in this body, and will allow us to be free from the binding effect of any situation in this world. In other words, for those of us who attain this state of awareness, no matter what may occur in life, we look at this planet as if we are but a tourist traveling through a foreign country. We may be here, but we know it is all temporary. We may try to do something to help if there is a tragedy, or spread the seeds of spiritual knowledge, but we also know that our own existence will soon be elsewhere, at least in due time. Nothing lasts forever, except that which is beyond the temporary, that which is spiritual in nature. And that is what we should cling to. That is what keeps us free. That is what gives us the happiness for which we have always sought. Now that we have found it, or have the chance to attain it, we should not let it slip away.

So, in our normal constitutional position as a spiritual being, free from this body and material consciousness, the living entity is fully satisfied and focused in spiritual bliss. It is this state that is called *brahma-bhuta* or *atma-nandi*, the state of self-satisfaction. It is only when we become conditioned by material contact and identify our physical body as being our real identity that we lose the *atma-nandi* state of being. It is then when we express ourselves through the means of lust, anger, jealousy, greed, and innumerable bodily desires. After that, the trouble begins.[3] This is why, in essence, everyone is hungry for real spiritual satisfaction. Everyone is looking for happiness, there is no doubt about that. But the only happiness that touches the soul is that which is connected with the spiritual dimension.

We all know there are two kinds of happiness. One is material happiness, which is the goal of those who are materially engrossed in seeking ways to satisfy the mind and senses. When one grows tired of being the servant of the senses, which are never totally satisfied, one reaches the stage of thirsting for real happiness and contentment, which can only be attained through spiritual satisfaction, the second type of happiness. The only means to reach this is through spiritual activities that directly affect the soul, which is our real identity, beyond the dictates of the mind and senses.[4]

Because the living being is covered by the material body and does not see the happiness that exists within his Self, he runs after happiness that is thought to be elsewhere, which is in connection with the material world. This process can be compared to trying to quench one's thirst by some other means than drinking water. You may find so many things and activities to occupy your mind, but in the end you are still thirsty. It is like a bird in a cage. You may do all you can for the cage, but if you neglect the bird inside, the bird will still need attention or will die. Similarly, we may be engaged in a multitude of thoughts and actions, yet in the end our soul is still waiting for us to bring our attention to the real needs in life, which are spiritual. Certainly, we must feed and clothe the body. These are real needs. Yet, since the body and everything connected with it are temporary, with a beginning and end, the real needs are more than that, more than bodily concerns. They are for that which does not die, which is eternal. Thus, that which is within is waiting for you to focus your attention to it. Until then, material happiness tends to be fleeting. It may last a while, but often leaves us still looking for additional fulfillment, or wondering why we are not completely satisfied.[5]

Basically, in order to be content with materialistic activities as the basis of one's pleasure, you must forget your real identity as a spiritual being. You must become so engrossed with the external situation around you that you forget or mislead yourself from looking within. Unfortunately, this forgetfulness of our real identity paves the way for desires for the body, and the emotions that follow, such as greed, anger, jealousy, and the fear of death.[6] However, that need to look within will wait for you and at some point come out in some other way. That is when in the midst of life, an event or tragedy may manifest which will force you to look at things in a different way. At that point you may suddenly begin to understand how you need to change, or what more you need to add to your life in order to make a difference to yourself, or a difference to those around you as well. You need to add some substance to your life, spiritual substance.

As we proceed with this line of thought, maybe you can begin to realize now that happiness or distress through the material senses has little meaning.[7] It can take a person years, or even lifetimes, before he or she perceives the fact that pleasure from the senses alone is not what gives real happiness. The distress or happiness that is determined by the mind has little reality because they come and go continually. Real happiness is never interrupted, nor is it temporary because it is related to the eternal soul. Once our material senses are purified, then our spiritual senses are revealed. It is through these which we can experience spiritual exhilaration and joy.[8]

This is why it is further explained that after having attained the human platform, if one simply engages in fruitive activities that often necessitate great struggles and are meant only to increase the pleasure of the senses, all of which are impermanent and have little substance for the soul, then that person is considered to have been cheated. He is cheated out of a valuable life and given only temporary prizes and sensations that disappear with time, or are inherited and enjoyed by someone else when he dies. The human life is considered a valuable boat that can take one to the realm of true happiness. It can deliver one to complete freedom from all materialistic limitations and further cycles of birth and death.[9]

This is one key point to consider, that even if people achieve material happiness, they do not know how to avoid death.[10] A prime factor in disturbing the plans of the materialists is this great interruption called death. It puts an end to everything that one has worked to attain. Thus, it is a cause of great disappointment for those who are so attached to this world that they do not want to leave. And this is a major deterrent for one's spiritual progress.

For this reason it is advised that if one wants to be truly happy, one's life should not be totally aimed for material gain or gratification of the senses. This does not have the capacity to make a sensible person happy. One should strive for a life of simplicity, few complications, self-preservation, good health, and work to assist others, especially those who are less fortunate or struggling with life. Beyond this, one must practice spiritual life to reconnect with one's higher Self on the spiritual platform.

The key point to understand is that once one knows the misery that hides in material existence, one should work to be free from the implications that may complicate one's life and engage in those spiritual practices that allow one to rise above the unhappiness that the ever-changing world can give. This happiness is found within, ever-existing in the Self, free from all the turmoil or confusion that lies in the externals around us. The spiritual living entity is naturally transcendental to material existence. It is only the false ego, the misidentification that one is the temporary material body, that makes one think that this material world is our real home, wherein we can make a situation so we can be totally happy and completely fulfilled.[11] There may, indeed, be moments of contentment in material activities, but one should not work simply for the fleeting moments of pleasure, but for the ultimate goal of bringing oneself to a higher plane of consciousness wherein there is the natural happiness of the higher spiritual Self. By adding this sort of real substance to one's life, one can reach a level of complete and never-ending joy and fulfillment.[12] This is the value and need for adding the spiritual path to one's life.

□

8

The Key to Real Happiness

GETTING BACK TO OUR SPIRITUAL NATURE

If you have read the previous chapters in this book, you will no doubt realize by now that getting back to our spiritual nature is the key that unlocks the door for finding the real way to happiness. It is not in material life but in uplifting ourselves to rise above it where independent happiness is found, and helping others to do the same. This is the best way of assisting others to be relieved of suffering and miseries. Of course, in places like America, there may be many people who feel that they are not suffering at all. They are happily working for their own material happiness, and for the benefit of their families, which actually is an extension of their own source of material pleasure. This is alright, and a responsibility that one must not neglect. Yet, as I have explained, families gradually grow up and leave the home to start their own centers of activity, their own families, with their own sources of concern. So where does that leave the senior citizens who no longer have a close network of emotional support? If they have not worked in a direct spiritual manner to reach inward to their higher Selves, then their happiness still depends on whatever comforts they have around them. And obviously everyone gets old, which generally means that the facility for pleasure and physical happiness decreases, and the body begins to show its wear and tear in the form of disease and difficulties. Anyone can see that as you age you cannot always do what you did when you were younger. So what does this mean?

One key point here is that, as it is explained in one of the ancient books of wisdom from the East, the *Srimad-Bhagavatam* (9.24.58), the Supreme Being acts in a most compassionate way through His material energies in the process of the creation, maintenance and annihilation of this cosmic manifestation to encourage the living beings to rise above the material platform of life and return to the spiritual domain, beyond the repetition of birth, disease, old age and death. It is not that the Lord has created the material worlds for the suffering of the living entities within it. However, such suffering will go on for those who are materially conditioned and attached to the various forms of temporary glitter in material existence. That cannot be helped. But again we need to remember that such pleasures without connection to reality, or to the relevance of our real identity as spiritual beings, is not and can never be permanent. Materialistic happiness is only related to our transitory mind and senses, which we have already discussed. And this neglects the natural and ever-existing happiness found within.

Another point to understand is that when we wish to enjoy in a way that is forgetful or separate from God, or according to our own selfish program, then we are placed into the world of duality, which means under the control of the mind and senses. Some aspects of this form of existence may seem pleasant enough, but one must accept the whole package, not just a small segment of it. Thus, one is left to endure so many difficulties that go on in this world, along with the continuous cycle of rebirth in a temporary body with relationships that must be given up whenever there is a need to relinquish the material body that we have.[1]

So again and again the Supreme Being sends various messengers, or even appears in this world, to deliver the necessary instructions for the living entities to be relieved of this situation. But such instructions are not forced on anyone. It is based on free will. So if one takes them to heart, he can be relieved of the material limitations and rise above them to the realm of spiritual happiness. However, for those who remain convinced that life in the material world and the fleeting moments of pleasure it provides is the best way to go, then they are allowed to stay in this world for as long as they like to deal with things as best they can.

Only after many lifetimes in the rounds of birth and death in the material world does such a conditioned soul begin to ask why they are not happy. They may ask what more is there that they may be missing? Or what do they have to do to feel really fulfilled? This is the same sort of questions that have often been asked by those who have become our greatest spiritual teachers. These questions signify that one is finally entering the human stage of life, the *vijnanamaya* stage. This is the doorway through which one may go to enter the truly spiritual platform of life, known as the *anandamaya* stage.

We have to understand that since we are spiritual beings, our connection with the spiritual strata is natural. This also means that our association with the material realm is only a temporary appearance. It does not provide everlasting fulfillment simply because it cannot. One reason is because everything in the material realm is a creation, which also means it has an end. Because everything is created in this place, we have no experience of eternity, bliss and knowledge in full. Whereas in the spiritual world, everything is eternally existent; nothing is merely created as we are used to seeing in the material realm. Furthermore, because of the absence of the material qualities in the spiritual domain, everything is eternal, full of bliss and knowledge. In this way, it provides the atmosphere for which we are always hankering, in which we can be fully satisfied.

Another difference is that the material energy acts as a covering of our spiritual identity and of the spiritual nature of everything else. This is to provide the illusory playground which allows the conditioned souls the means by which they can pretend to be something other than what they really are, and also to forget about God if they want. Yet, in the spiritual realm there is no such covering. Thus, there is no forgetfulness of our real spiritual identities, and no forgetfulness of our eternal nature of engaging in transcendental loving service to the Supreme. Again, this is why when we engage in the service of helping others, especially if we see them as children of God, we also receive a joy that can be higher than those who are being helped, and especially higher than simply serving our own mind and senses. That is because such service is a reflection of our natural spiritual position.[2]

This is also why those who have attained, or nearly attained, the spiritual strata are peaceful with little or no material hankering. While those who are completely liberated from material influences have no such demands for sensual or mental happiness whatsoever. They are focused on their spiritual identity and desire only to help others in attaining a similar peaceful situation and service to God.[3] In this way, the real happiness that we are all striving for is achieved by attaining a spiritual existence.[4] And this can be accomplished in our present situation.

THE WAY FOR ATTAINING A SPIRITUAL EXISTENCE

While learning the means of spiritual awakening, there are many guidelines that help direct us toward this state of awareness. First, one should give up attachment to the ways of serving the five senses and recognize the unnecessary endeavors in which one is forced to participate when motivated in a such a way. One should also tolerate the duality of pleasure and pain, knowing that they are like the passing of the winter and summer seasons. Also, undergoing voluntary simplicity and austerity helps to keep your life uncomplicated for inquiring further into the higher avenues of Truth. This does not mean to avoid the responsibilities that you may have already accepted, or leave your family. However, you must keep things simple so that the affairs of life do not become so demanding or complicated that it leaves you with no time for peace or the pursuit of your spiritual inquisitiveness and advancement. The advice is given in the *Srimad-Bhagavatam* (7.14.6) where it says that an intelligent man should keep his own program of activities very simple. Even if others amongst his friends or family offer suggestions, he should externally agree, but internally remain determined to not create a cumbersome existence in which he fails to fulfill the purpose of life.

As you proceed, give up enmity toward others, and look upon everyone equally as spiritual beings.

Practice to not identify your Self with your body and surroundings, and in this way subdue anger and lamentation toward whatever happens in your existence. Reduce unnecessary talks with those who are materially motivated, or who will instill their own materialistic and sensual desires in you. And, if necessary, observe more seclusion in order to help control the mind and senses. As you progress along this road, look for like-minded people with whom you can associate. Inquire from other seekers of Truth and devotees of the Lord to share insights and realizations. Everyday read the revealed scriptures that will invoke your devotions and bless you with higher levels of spiritual knowledge. This is also an important form of association. Continue to practice your devotional activities (*bhakti-yoga*) and your thinking and meditating on the Supreme Lord. Through patience and enthusiasm you will become elevated in knowledge and realizations.[5]

Furthermore, since it is explained that we are all born in ignorance yet must reawaken the spiritual knowledge within us, we must take instruction from those more advanced than ourselves who can help us understand the process for achieving that enlightened state. If we can accept direction from a proper spiritual authority, then we can also become free from the illusion, or our misconceptions of life, although situated within this material world.[6]

One should also begin to view death without fear, and define the body as different from the soul.

One should not enjoy the bodily necessities of life in exaggeration. However, when one realizes the true nature of the Self, one can move about the world free from attachment. This is due to having right vision, and seeing one's body as part of the temporary or illusory energy. In this way, one deals only with what is necessary in keeping body and soul together, yet remains unconcerned with the material world and becomes free from its miseries.[7]

By cultivating a spiritual mentality and seeing that all material objects are merely displays of the energy of God, one can give up the attraction of thinking such objects are merely for our sensual enjoyment. This will continue to remind us of the beauty and power of the Supreme.[8] It is through this means that we direct our attraction to the source of all beauty, energy and love, the Supreme Being.

By this means, it is explained that the surest way of escaping from the influence of material existence is to begin engaging in the devotional service of the Lord, who is the ultimate shelter of all saintly persons, through the process of associating with the Lord's devotees.[9] This is the essence of spiritual life. Knowing that invoking our natural loving nature toward the Supreme is the way to the highest happiness, then of what use are extra endeavors of religious pursuit, such as the yoga system, philosophical speculation, renunciation of the world, severe austerities, etc., if it does not awaken our love of God?[10] And the real goal of love of God is to enjoy spiritual bliss.[11] Furthermore, one cannot enjoy transcendental ecstasy until he is relieved from the materialistic concerns of life.[12]

In this way, it can be recognized that the real form of spiritual realization is achieving the state of spontaneous devotional service to the Supreme. This invokes a bliss that can be fully satisfying when in contact with the Supreme Being in any number of ways. The reason is that the soul has an eternal nature, which is to serve the Supreme Soul. This is naturally awakened through the process of *bhakti-yoga*, or connecting with the Supreme through the means of devotional love.[13] Even if one's mind is too absorbed in activities for material pursuits, it can be engaged in the service of the Supreme and become fixed in full spiritual consciousness. Thus, the mind, being freed from activities for sensual pleasure, becomes progressively spiritualized.[14] The process of *bhakti-yoga* can also cut the knot of *karma* as well, thus freeing us from the bondage of reactions of our past fruitive work or other selfish activities, and allowing us to continue in our spiritual progress without such hindrances.[15] Once we take shelter of the Lord through the serious practice of devotion, *bhakti*, we can be completely cleansed, and such a person never comes back to this material existence, which is full of the threefold miseries.[16]

The simplest process for such success on the spiritual path is recommended as the constant chanting of the Lord's holy names. As stated in the

Srimad-Bhagavatam (2.1.11): "O King, constant chanting of the holy name of the Lord [such as in the Hare Krishna mantra] after the ways of the great authorities is the doubtless and fearless way of success for all, including those who are free from all material desires, those who are desirous of all material enjoyment, and also those who are self-satisfied by dint of transcendental knowledge."

It is further clarified that "The Absolute Truth is Sri Krishna [the form and personality of God known as the most loving], and loving devotion to Sri Krishna exhibited in pure love is achieved through congregational chanting of the holy name, which is the essence of bliss." (*Caitanya-caritamrita, Adi-lila*, 1.96)

The basis is that there are only three things which are eternal. One is God, the second is the living beings, and the third is the relationship between them, which is love, specifically eternal spiritual love. Everything else is temporary. This is why when we find love in the material world, which is the highest pleasure to be found here, we feel most happy. It is only because it is a mere reflection of the spiritual love that we are naturally craving, specifically that love between ourselves and the Supreme Being. Naturally, we share a spiritual love with all of His parts and parcels, the other spiritual beings. But such love is manifested to its fullest on the spiritual strata. That is why we are never really fulfilled while trying to find love within the material domain. It is never all that we want. It is limited. Therefore, the spiritual world is where the love which we instinctively pursue is manifested to its fullest. That is what the spiritual world is for.

The ultimate state of loving happiness can only be attained within a relationship centered on the Supreme Being. It is He who is also the Supreme Lover, the source of all happiness and emotional reciprocation. Once the Lord is the center of our relations, there will be no other love that can compare. It is, indeed, the basis for the happiness for which we are always seeking.

ENJOYING THE PLEASURE WITHIN

Once a person is enlightened to a higher state of awareness, and especially after reaching a spiritual level of consciousness, he sees himself as transcendental to the body, although living within it. It is like awakening from a dream and no longer identifying with the body and the experience he had while dreaming. Furthermore, he knows that the body may perform actions, but he, as the spiritual being within, is not directly in contact with the objects that the senses perceive. It is only the vehicle of the body which performs the materialistic bodily activities.[17]

Even if one is completely liberated while living on this earthly plane of existence, he or she accepts the body as a vehicle given according to one's past desires and *karma*, which are the consequences to a person's behavior in the past. Thus, whatever good or bad fortune that may arise, such a person accepts it as the reactions from past pious or impious activities. Remaining firm in his understanding, he works in a way that reduces whatever opportunity there might be to acquire another material body, and then again find himself in a similar situation in the next life.[18]

The point of this awareness is that the person in the state of spiritual realization keeps higher knowledge (that he is a spiritual being and a part of the Supreme) and detachment in perspective, while maintaining his devotional practice. While seeing everything in this correct point of view, he not only becomes less affected by the material existence, but it also has less influence over him.[19] As one becomes freer from the effects of the material energy, he or she can become freed from the common emotions of lamentation and hankering. These emotions are the cause of so many self-imposed problems in which the majority of people often find themselves. It is the single most limiting factor in why people cannot tune into the happiness within. One who is attached to material circumstances cannot enjoy the inner happiness of the higher Self. Thus, he remains focused on trying to be happy by working to rearrange the circumstances around him. Therefore, it is advised that if one can tolerate the urges of the material senses and, thus, reduce the force of desire and anger, he can reach that state of real happiness in this world.[20]

A person who is spiritually focused, however, is not so attracted to the variegated forms of temporary material sense pleasure. He or she is concentrated on the higher Self and the Supreme Being, the source of all eternal and real happiness. In this way, such a person enjoys unlimited happiness, enjoying the pleasure within.[21]

Another key point to understand is that we may say that certain people or things are the cause of our mental or physical happiness or distress, but where does the soul fit into this conception? One cannot relish mental or bodily happiness, nor feel unhappiness, without identifying oneself as the physical body. Therefore, this pleasure and pain caused by other people or objects are merely interactions between bodies. It is within the illusion, or our misconception of who and what we are. Such misidentification is also the cause for so many other pains that naturally come simply because of being within a material body. So, when we understand this, why should we become angry with oneself or others when real happiness is actually beyond the false bodily conception?

To explain further, since the body has life only because of the soul within it, it is not the actual recipient of happiness or distress. The soul does not participate in material happiness or anguish because it is wholly spiritual. The soul has its own source of happiness that is completely independent of material circumstances. All we need to do is enable ourselves to tap into that direct source of spiritual happiness. A person who truly understands and perceives this has nothing to fear from the material creation, or whatever happens within it.[22] By clearly understanding the temporary and illusory nature of material things, one should remain detached from depending on such impermanent forms of happiness. By continuing to be aware that the world is not the ultimate reality, even if one involves himself with the material energy, one will remain free from falling into illusion, or again depending on such fleeting sources for one's happiness and the distress that follows.[23]

In this way, one should be satisfied with whatever happiness comes due to destiny and cultivate spiritual consciousness to enjoy life through the transcendental senses. "In the spiritually joyous state, one is situated in boundless transcendental happiness and enjoys himself through transcendental senses. Established thus, one never departs from the Truth." (*Bhagavad-gita* 6.21)

These spiritual senses are underneath the material covering of the body. We can experience life to its fullest and attain true happiness once we are able to uncover these spiritual senses and engage them in their natural activity and desires. This is the devotional service to the Lord and His devotees,

His parts and parcels. Then the spiritual senses and the soul will be truly content and satisfied. Without this, no matter how we try to make ourselves happy, genuine and lasting bliss and contentment will not be possible while on the material platform, which itself is conditional and fleeting.[24] Being a servant of the Supreme, and using our inner senses in His service, is the constitutional position of all living beings. This is the way all living entities can be completely satisfied, just as a child is fully content while in the arms of a loving father or mother.

HAPPINESS FROM THE SPIRITUAL PATH

Even before one becomes completely spiritualized or liberated, simply following the path toward transcendental consciousness provides one with glimpses of the highest forms of happiness. The spiritual path is not the opiate of the people, which ignorant and foolish people may say. It is the means by which we can allow the direct engagement of the soul in spiritual activity. In fact, the Supreme Being Himself, as Lord Krishna, states that one whose mind is fixed on Him attains the highest happiness. By virtue of one's identity with the spiritual domain, he is liberated, and his mind is peaceful. His passions become quieted and he is freed from sin.[25]

Herein it is hinted that the ultimate aim of religion is to attain the life of complete freedom on the spiritual platform, and free oneself from material bondage or karmic reactions that will force us to accept continued births and deaths.[26] This freedom is also displayed in the soul being able to engage in its natural activities of devotion to God. Actually, as stated in *Srimad-Bhagavatam* (1.2.22), since time immemorial, all serious transcendentalists render loving devotion to the Lord, Krishna, with great delight because such service is enlivening to the Self.

This is actually what we all want. We want to be enlivened and enthused. It is just that so many look for such thrills in the association of material sense objects within the impermanent material energy. It is like looking for love in all the wrong places. Thus, true enlivenment is what is needed.

The real path to such freedom and enthusiasm, as explained in the Eastern texts, is *bhakti-yoga*, devotional service to the Lord, Krishna. Due to the spiritual constitutional position of the soul, the supreme occupation of all living beings is that by which they can attain the loving devotional service of God, the Supreme Soul. Such unmotivated and uninterrupted service is all that can completely satisfy the Self.[27] Nothing else can give such satisfaction to the soul. The reason is that devotional service to the Lord is the chief function of the living being.[28] And we can see that. Look around and you can notice that everyone is serving something. Parents serve their children, later children serve their parents, husbands and wives serve each other, we all serve the government by paying taxes, people serve their bosses at work, and on and on. So service cannot be stopped. That is our natural position. However, we can change the direction of that service. We may get some joy out of serving the Lord's parts and parcels while in the material realm, such as our wife, husband, children, relatives, friends, etc. Yet to directly serve the Supreme Being offers the highest emotional taste and most intense reciprocation. It all depends on how deep into it we go.

It is explained that "The conception of servitude to Sri Krishna generates such an ocean of joy in the soul that even the joy of oneness with the Absolute, if multiplied ten million times, could not compare to a drop of it... Nowhere else is there such joy as that which is tasted in this emotion of servitude. The most beloved goddess of fortune resides on the chest of Sri Krishna, yet she too, earnestly praying, begs for the joy of service at His feet. All the associates of Lord Krishna, such as Brahma, Shiva, Narada, Shuka and Sanatana, are very much pleased in the sentiment of servitude." (*Caitanya-caritamrita, Adi-lila,* 6.44-47) Through these descriptions we can understand that for the soul there is no higher bliss than the loving devotional emotions to the Supreme.

It is further explained by Srila Jiva Gosvami in his *Pritisandarbha* that only such devotional service can lead one to meet the Supreme Lord face to face. The reason is that although the Lord is completely self-satisfied, and needs nothing else from anyone, He nonetheless becomes attracted to the devotional emotions of His devotees, and thus reveals Himself to the devotee because of such devotional service. Thus, the ultimate level of Vedic knowledge and all religious understanding rests in knowing the science of performing devotional service, whereby one's spiritual emotions are developed.[29] When these emotions are established, one can focus on the pastimes of the Supreme and be happy all the time. This is more fully explained in the *Caitanya-caritamrita* (*Cc. Antya-lila*, 5.47): "Tasting the transcendental, effulgent, sweetly ecstatic love of Krishna, such a person can enjoy life twenty-four hours a day in the transcendental bliss of the sweetness of Krishna's pastimes." Such happiness in feeling the reciprocation from the Supreme Being Himself compares with nothing else, as we discuss in the following segment.

HAPPINESS IN THE RECIPROCATION WITH THE SUPREME

The Supreme Lord has promised to reciprocate with His devotees according to the way they worship and surrender to Him. Therefore, as we submit to the will of the Supreme, He will reward us to that degree. Thus, as we give pleasure to the Lord by our devotional emotions and activities, He will also reciprocate with us to the degree of our love for

Him, or even more so.[30] In this way, one is happiest when simply depending on the Lord.

It is stated that Lord Krishna is happiness personified. Therefore, the pleasure that His pure devotees experience is manifest from the Lord's own pleasure potency.[31] Even Lord Krishna says that for those who are without any personal sensual desires, who are peaceful, without false ego and merciful to all living entities, and whose minds are always focused on Him, they enjoy in Him a happiness that cannot be known or achieved in any other way.[32]

In this regard, Lord Krishna Himself says that by the unalloyed devotional service rendered to Him by His devotees brings Him under their control. He cannot be controlled in this way by any other process, including mystic yoga, pious work, Vedic study, religious philosophy, austerity, or renunciation. Only by practicing unalloyed devotional service with full faith in Him can one obtain the Supreme Lord.[33] Therefore, by the process of spiritual engagement in devotional service, the Lord directly reciprocates with the surrendered devotees, who then experience a happiness that knows no bounds.

Thus, even while in this material world, all forms of happiness that so many people take so seriously are actually very small compared to the great ocean of bliss in the reciprocation that one receives from the Lord, or especially from directly seeing Lord Krishna, which is indeed possible in so many ways. To describe this feeling, Sri Caitanya Mahaprabhu also exclaimed, "Unalloyed love of Krishna is like the ocean of happiness. If someone gets one drop of it, the whole world can drown in that drop." (*Cc.* Madhya-lila, 2.49)

In conclusion, it is described in the *Srimad-Bhagavatam* (2.6.36) that even the Supreme Lord Krishna cannot measure the limits of His own expansion or the happiness that is coming from Him simply because it is always unlimitedly increasing. Therefore, it is advised that the best that one can do is to surrender unto His lotus feet, which alone can deliver one from the miseries of repeated birth and death, and allow one to perceive all happiness. This is the key to attaining real happiness.

□

Chapter Notes

In most of the chapters, when I am explaining things, it is not only my opinion or experience that I'm relating, but I also include specific information found in some of the authentic Vedic texts of the East, such as *Srimad-Bhagavatam* (*Bhag*), or *Bhagavad-gita* (*Bg*), or *Caitanya-caritamrita* (*Cc*). These are known for having some of the highest levels of spiritual understanding. The following is the list of references that are noted in the previous chapters.

CHAPTER 4

1. (*Srimad-Bhagavatam* 6.10.9-10)
2. (*Bhag*.11.23.17 & 20-21)
3. (*Bhag*.10.10.8)
4. (*Bhag*.11.23.18-19)
5. (*Bhag*.11.23.16)
6. (*Bhag*.7.13.32 & 34)
7. (*Bhag*.11.23.15)
8. (*Bhag*.7.14.8)
9. (*Bhag*.8.19.37)
10. (*Bhag*.8.22.26-27)

CHAPTER 5

1. (*Bhag*. 10.49.20)
2. (*Bhag*. 7.6.9)
3. (*Bhag*. 1.15.37)
4. (*Bhag*. 3.30.17-19)
5. (*Bhag*. 4.25.4)
6. (*Bhag*. 6.17.29)
7. (*Bhag*. 11.8.1)
8. (*Bhag*. 6.17.30)
9. (*Bhag*. 4.29.2B)
10. (*Bhag*. 7.9.25)

CHAPTER 6

1. (*Bhag*. 11.10.31)
2. (*Bhag*. 1.3.33)
3. (*Bhag*. 1.15.31)
4. (*Bhag*. 2.1.15)
5. (*Bhag*. 11.11.1 pur.)
6. (*Bhag*. 11.23.59)
7. (*Bhag*. 4.9.33)
8. (*Bhag*. 10.51.47)
9. (*Bhag*. 1.11.3)
10. (*Bhag*. 11.13.9-11)
11. (*Bhag*. 4.28.20. pur.)
12. (*Bhag*. 8.19.21)
13. (*Bhag*. 7.6.14 & 7.5.31)
14. (*Bhag*. 4.25.6)
15. (*Bhag*. 4.29.29-31)
16. (*Bhag*. 11.7.52)

CHAPTER 7

1.(*Bhag*. 3.30.9)
2.(*Bhag*. 1.2.8 pur.)

3.(*Bhag*. 1.2.19)
4.(*Bhag*. 1.12.6 pur.)
5.(*Bhag*. 7.13.29)
6.(*Bhag*. 3.12.2)
7.(*Bhag*. 7.2.48)
8.(*Bhag*. 1.13.17 pur.)
9.(*Bhag*. 4.23.28)
10.(*Bhag*. 11.10.9)
11.(*Bhag*. 4.29.25 pur.)
12.(*Bhag*. 1.5.18)

CHAPTER 8

1. (*Bhag*. 9.24.58)
2. (*Cc. Adi-lila* 5, v22)
3. (*Bhag*. 3.2.15)
4. (*Bhag*. 1.19.4)
5. (*Bhag*. 5.5.10-13)
6. (*Bhag*. 3.33.10)
7. (*Bhag*. 3.31.47-48)
8. (*Bhag*. 11.13.25 pur.)
9. (*Bhag*. 11.11.48)
10. (*Bhag*. 4.31.12)
11. (*Cc. Madhya-lila* 20, v142)
12. (*Cc. Madhya-lila* 7, v126)
13. (*Cc. Adi-lila* 1, v91)
14. (*Bhag*. 2.1.18)
15. (*Bhag*. 1.2.15)
16. (*Bhag*. 4.21.32)
17. (*Bhag*. 11.11.8-9)
18. (*Bhag*. 5.1.16)
19. (*Bhag*. 3.25.18)
20. (*Bhag*. Bg.5.23)
21. (*Bg*. 5.21)

22. (*Bhag*. 11.23.50-56)
23. (*Bhag*. 11.13.35)
24. (*Bhag*. 8.19.24)
25. (*Bg*.6.27)
26. (*Bhag*. 1.2.25)
27. (*Bhag*. 1.2.6)
28. (*Cc. Madhya-lila*, 22 v17)
29. (*Cc. Adi-lila* 4, v60)
30. (*Cc. Adi-lila* 4, v177)
31. (*Cc. Madhya-lila* 8, v158)
32. (*Bhag*. 11.14.17)
33. (*Bhag*. 11.14.20-21)

□

Glossary

Bhagavad-gita—the Song of God, the essence of Vedic spiritual knowledge, spoken by Lord Krishna to His devotee Arjuna. *Bhakti*--love and devotion for God.

Bhakti-yoga—the path of developing and offering pure devotional service to the Supreme.

Caitanya-caritamrta—the scripture by Krishnadasa Kaviraja which explains the teachings and pastimes of Lord Caitanya Mahaprabhu. *Caitanya Mahaprabhu*--considered the most recent incarnation of the Lord who appeared in the 15th century in Bengal and who originally started the *sankirtana* movement, based on congregational chanting of the holy names.

Hare—the Lord's pleasure potency, Radharani, who is approached for accessibility to the Lord.

Karma—material actions performed for developing one's position or for future results which produce *karmic* reactions that one must endure in the future.

Karma-yoga—system of yoga for using one's activities for spiritual advancement.

Krishna—the name of the Supreme Person, meaning the all-attractive.

Maha-mantra—the best *mantra* for self-realization in this age, called the Hare Krishna *mantra*, which is Hare Krishna, Hare Krishna, Krishna Krishna, Hare Hare/Hare Rama, Hare Rama, Rama Rama, Hare Hare. This allows the listener or chanter to associate with the Supreme through His names and the spiritual vibrations within them.

Mantra—a sound vibration which prepares the mind for spiritual realization and delivers the mind from material inclinations. In some cases a *mantra* is chanted for specific material benefits.

Srimad-Bhagavatam—the most ripened fruit of the tree of Vedic knowledge compiled by Vyasadeva.

Three-fold miseries—those miseries caused by the body itself, those caused by other beings, and those caused by nature.

□

References

The following is the list of the Vedic texts that were referred to or directly quoted to explain some of the knowledge and information presented in this book.

Bhagavad-gita As It Is, translated with purports by A.C. Bhaktivedanta Swami, Bhaktivedanta Book Trust, New York/Los Angeles, 1972.

Brihan-naradiya Purana,

Caitanya-caritamrita, translation and purports by A.C. Bhaktivedanta Swami, Bhaktivedanta Book Trust, Los Angeles, 1974.

Caitanya Upanisad, translated by Kusakratha dasa, Bala Books, New York, 1970.

Mahabharata, Kamala Subramaniam, Bharatiya Vidya Bhavan, Bombay, 1982.

Pritisandarbha, Srila Jiva Gosvami.

Srimad-Bhagavatam, translation and purports by A.C. Bhaktivedanta Swami, Bhaktivedanta Book trust, New York/Los Angeles, 1972.

The Upanishads, translated by Swami Prabhavananda and Frederick Manchester, New American Library, New York, 1957.

Twelve Essential Upanishads, Tridandi Sri Bhakti Prajnan Yati, Sree Gaudiya Math, Madras, 1982.

□□□